'You care to

His glance trail... down to rest laz... endearing qualit... lead you to heartache, your compassion shines through. No wonder your small patients love you.'

His mouth brushed hers, gently, coaxingly, exploring the soft contours of her lips with a tender expertise that made her senses whirl.

She heard him mutter hoarsely, 'This has to be madness,' but he lifted her closer, kissing her with a deepening passion that took her breath away.

When **Joanna Neil** discovered Mills & Boon®, her life-long addiction to reading crystallised into an exciting new career writing medical romances. Her characters are probably the outcome of her varied lifestyle, which has included working as a clerk, typist, nurse, and infant teacher. She enjoys dressmaking and cooking at her home in Leicestershire, England. Her family includes a husband, son and daughter, an exuberant yellow Labrador and two slightly crazed cockatiels.

Recent titles by the same author:

PRACTISING PARTNERS

THE CHILDREN'S DOCTOR

BY

JOANNA NEIL

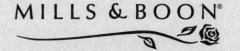

MILLS & BOON®

*First published in Great Britain 2001
Harlequin Mills & Boon Limited,
Eton House, 18-24 Paradise Road, Richmond, Surrey TW9 1SR*

© Joanna Neil 2001

ISBN 0 263 82713 5

*Set in Times Roman 10½ on 12½ pt.
03-0102-46247*

*Printed and bound in Spain
by Litografia Rosés, S.A., Barcelona*

CHAPTER ONE

THE sound of a steel band drifted across the deserted cove, a relaxed and dreamily heady tempo that seemed to invite the tapping of feet and the rhythmic swaying of hips. Listening to it, Anna smiled. Wasn't this what the Caribbean was all about?

She breathed in deeply, soaking up the sights and sounds, absorbing the atmosphere all around her. A tropical heat haze shimmered over the golden sand, and there was only the faintest breeze to stir the fronds of the palm trees fringing the beach. It made her thankful that she had chosen to wear just a skimpy cotton top and a skirt that swathed her hips and left a good deal of her legs bare.

The music must be coming from the other side of the headland, she decided, scanning the horizon. At the far end of the cove, a limestone bluff thrust its way into the sea, and she could see numerous small inlets which had been formed there by the weathering of the crags over time. The ground below was strewn with rocks, adding a touch of grandeur to the landscape.

As she looked around, she suddenly became aware of snatches of a different sound being carried on the air, one that mingled with the lively throb of steel drums and made her pause for a moment to listen more intently. What was it?

She frowned. It wasn't the sound of the sea…that was too calm, surely, with waves lapping at the shore in desultory fashion, breaking up into lacy ribbons of white foam that melted away almost as soon as they had formed. No, it was something else that she had heard.

Then, with a faint sense of shock, she made out a muffled sobbing, like that of a child in pain. The sound squeezed at her heart and spurred her into action, driving her to anxiously search amongst the boulders to find out where it was coming from.

After a while, hidden behind a large rock, she came across the huddled form of a small boy. He looked as though he had hurt himself, and instantly compassion washed through her like a tide, making her want to hug him to her.

'Oh, you poor little thing,' she murmured softly, bending down beside the child. 'What's wrong, sweetheart? Have you hurt yourself?'

He couldn't have been much more than three years old, about the same age as her nephew, and she felt an overwhelming rush of sympathy for him. Concern, too. What on earth was he doing out here, alone?

'Shall I have a look at you and see if I can do anything to help?'

The little boy stopped crying for a moment, staring at Anna with wide brown eyes that seemed to grow larger with every second, but he didn't say a word.

She smiled encouragingly. His reaction to her didn't surprise her very much…he was only little and he was right to be wary of strangers.

This little boy had warm golden skin tones and

black hair that hugged his head in a mass of tiny springy curls. He was very much like Daniel in his colouring, and the knowledge tugged at her heart all over again.

'Is it your arm?' she asked, seeing the way that he was holding it, stiffly, as though moving it would have caused him more pain.

He nodded slowly, crying quietly again in soft little hiccups, but she was relieved to find that he understood what she was saying. She said carefully, 'What happened, can you tell me?'

'I felled over...' His lip began to tremble at the memory, and Anna put an arm around him in a comforting gesture, taking care not to put pressure on his shoulder. The collarbone looked slightly distorted, and her professional training told her that the long slender bone might have been broken. The collarbone was easily fractured in a fall onto the shoulder or an outstretched arm, and as a paediatrician she had come across the injury many times.

'I think you're being very brave,' she told him. 'Perhaps I can do something to help you. I'm Anna. What's your name?'

'Sebastian,' he lisped, choking down a convulsive sob. 'I want my mama... My arm hurts...'

'I know it does. We'll try to find her in a minute, I promise.' She soothed him quietly, holding him against her and lightly stroking his head until he was calmer. 'I think you might have snapped the bone in your shoulder,' she explained gently. 'That's why it's so painful, but it will mend, given time. A bandage might take the weight off it and help to make you feel a bit better. I'll see if I can find something in my bag that will do the trick, shall I?'

He didn't look too sure about that, but when she delved in her canvas bag and brought out one of the toy cars she had brought with her in case she managed to find Daniel, he looked at it curiously.

'Well, I never,' she said, looking at the shiny red sports car and feigning surprise. 'I wonder how that got in there? Here, would you like to play with it?'

She passed it to him while she searched for her silk scarf, and when she had retrieved the filmy square from the depths of the bag she quickly fashioned it into a figure-of-eight bandage, looping it carefully around his forearm and fastening the ends securely around his neck.

'There. Does that feel any better?'

He nodded slowly, still uncertain, but said politely, 'Yes…fank you.'

'Good. I'm glad.' As long as he was careful to keep the arm still, he shouldn't suffer too badly, but he ought to have some medication to relieve the pain, and that meant he would need to see his own doctor.

There was also a bump on his head and a slight graze, which needed checking out, and she would feel far happier if his parents were around to take care of him.

'Which way did you come, Sebastian? Do you remember?'

'From the party…over there.' With his free arm he pointed to a narrow inlet which cut into the headland and which Anna thought must lead to the next bay, the place where the music was coming from. The tide was out, and the passage through the rocks looked dry for the moment.

She frowned, turning back to the child. How could anyone be so selfish as to carry on partying and forget all about the boy? He was hardly more than a babe.

'I was going that way myself,' she told him. 'I'll take you back over there, and we'll see if we can find your mummy and daddy, shall we?' With any luck, they would already be out searching for him.

Sebastian's halting voice cut into her thoughts. 'Dada Carlos…' he said tremulously.

Anna guessed he still needed reassurance, and as she began to gently wipe his tear-stained face with a tissue from her bag, she repeated softly, 'Carlos… Is that your daddy?'

His eyes widened, shimmering still. 'Dada Carlos…' he said again, but happily this time. 'He's coming to fetch me…' And when she turned to follow the direction of his excited gaze, she was startled to see that a man was emerging onto the beach through an arch in the rock.

He stood for a moment, a tall, dark-haired man, silhouetted against the headland, his body lean and honed to physical perfection. Then he turned, his glance carefully searching the area until finally it came to rest on Anna and the boy. He started towards them.

He was long-limbed and lithe, Anna noticed, his movements supple and well co-ordinated as he stepped sure-footedly from rock to rock. He was wearing casual clothes—a T-shirt that spanned broad

shoulders and hugged a flat stomach, and light coloured trousers that faithfully moulded lean hips.

He came closer and Anna was able to see him more
clearly. His face was strong boned, firm jawed, his
features distinctively carved. She couldn't be sure and
he looked to be of European descent, but she guessed
there might be a Latin American streak. Like the
boy's, his skin was golden toned, but his hair was
different, crisply black, straight, short and attractively
styled.

Anna frowned. He was a man with responsibilities,
the father of a three-year-old child who should have
been kept under firm supervision. What was either
parent thinking of, leaving their son to his own devices, at the mercy of the rocks and the sea?

The man was within a few feet of them now, and
as he approached he cast a swift but thorough glance
over Anna before turning to the boy.

'So, here you are, Seb,' he said, his voice deep and
huskily accented. 'I've been looking for you. You
shouldn't have wandered off,' he added in a reproving
tone. 'We were very worried about you.'

Sebastian lowered his head, but said nothing until
Carlos, looking at the makeshift bandage, asked on a
concerned note, '*Qué pasa?* What happened to you?
Are you hurt?'

The boy's lip began to quiver all over again. 'I
wanted to look at the rock pools,' he managed, looking up at Carlos with tear filled eyes, 'but I
slipped…and I hurted my arm.' His little face crum-
pled.

The man bent to look at the shoulder, and then said,

'Poor lad, you are in a bad way, aren't you? But I can see that someone has bound it up for you. Was it your new friend who did this?'

Sebastian nodded solemnly. 'Anna maked it better…a bit… It's very hurting.'

He nodded. 'I can see that it still hurts.'

Carlos had been concentrating his attention on the boy so far, but now his glance shifted Anna's way, his gold-flecked eyes surveying her thoughtfully.

'It seems as though we're in your debt, Anna. It was good of you to take the time and trouble to stay with Sebastian and I'm very grateful to you for what you have done. You seemed to know exactly how to make him more comfortable, and we're both thankful for that.'

He sounded sincere enough, but Anna was still riled about his role in the affair and she wasn't going to allow herself to be sidetracked by his smooth manner. The man had neglected the infant and she wasn't about to let that pass without comment.

'There's no need to thank me. I would hardly stand by and do nothing, and I was glad to do what I could to help. It was upsetting, seeing him in such a state.' She paused, then added tautly, 'Perhaps if he hadn't been left to wander here on his own in the first place there would have been no need for me to step in.'

The tawny eyes flared and she wondered if her rebuke had scored a hit, but, instead of answering her, he looked down at the child once more, assessing him keenly.

Anna decided to press her point home. 'I think he has most likely broken his collarbone. The poor child is in a good deal of pain, you know, and he really ought to see a doctor as soon as possible.'

Carlos frowned as he brought his attention back to Anna. 'You're right. I'll see to it.'

'Good. I'm glad about that.' Sebastian was making little hiccuping sobs, and she guessed he was frightened, as much as anything, by what had happened to him. She cuddled him. 'I expect he'll need an X-ray, so that you can be sure of the extent of the damage,' she murmured.

He nodded. 'We'll go now.'

Anna gently stroked Seb's arm. Now that his father had arrived to take over from her, there was probably little more she could do for the boy, but she was very conscious of the child's trembling and she was feeling terribly reluctant to let go of him.

Seb looked up at her. 'You said you was coming with me,' he said haltingly, between his sobs, 'and we find my mama. I want you come with me.'

Carlos's glance shifted over both of them. 'Would you be able to come with us?' he asked. 'I think it would make Seb feel a lot better if you stayed. He's feeling hurt and probably he's frightened, too, and a little insecure just now.'

'I know,' she murmured. 'I guessed as much. Yes, I can come along with you.' She wanted to be sure that the child would be looked after properly. His father had shown little responsibility for the boy's welfare until now, and if she went with them she would feel as though she had done the right thing, and she would be certain that everything possible had been done to make him more comfortable.

She glanced towards the headland. 'I was going in that direction anyway. I was on my way to the harbour when I came across Seb.'

'*Bueno*. That's good. Thank you. It'll be much more reassuring for Seb if you're with us.'

The little boy managed a watery smile, and reached up to slip his free hand into hers. He looked up at her and whispered, 'Can I keep the car?'

Anna blinked in surprise. She had forgotten about the little red car. 'Of course you can keep it,' she said, and a tiny glimmer of relief came into the child's eyes.

Carlos's well-shaped mouth twitched into a wry smile. 'Three-year-olds obviously have very different priorities to us.' He reached down to lift the boy up, and she released him carefully into his arms. 'I'll carry you,' he told Seb quietly. 'We don't want to risk you taking another tumble, do we?'

He held him gently, taking care not to put pressure on the injured limb, and all three of them started to make their way across the beach to the bay on the other side of the promontory.

As they approached the archway in the rocks, the sound of music and laughter became louder.

Anna sent Carlos an oblique glance. 'Do you live close by?' she asked. 'I suppose you must, if Seb was right in saying that he had come from the party over there.'

'He was right,' he answered. 'Perhaps I should have introduced myself before this. I am Carlos Barrantes…my house overlooks the harbour.'

'I'm Anna Somerville,' she told him in return.

The rocks here were becoming precarious, and as she struggled to keep her balance he put out a hand to steady her, clasping her arm easily with his strong fingers. Her nerves sparked in response to his touch, and she forced herself to be calm. He was simply helping her out after all, and there was no need for her defences to go shooting to red alert.

'Were you celebrating a special occasion?'

'In a way. My friends and I are enjoying a small get-together this afternoon on the beach to celebrate a successful year... The harvests have been good, and business plans have gone well for the most part.' He sent her a sideways glance. 'And you? Were you planning on exploring the harbour, or are you headed for somewhere specific?'

'I was hoping to meet up with someone who lives near there,' she told him. She wasn't exactly sure where Nick's house was, but she could make enquiries some other time when she saw the lie of the land.

'Have we made you late?'

She shook her head. 'It doesn't matter. It wasn't a precise arrangement.'

In fact, Nick didn't even know that she was here. She was just hoping that her brother-in-law would be at home, and that she would be able to talk to him about her nephew, Daniel. She wasn't particularly looking forward to the meeting—he had never been the easiest of men to deal with, and this was no ordinary situation that she had to handle, was it? Was she up to it? She grimaced. The truth was, she had to make it work for her sister's sake.

By now they had reached the headland, and they

made their way through the narrow opening and onto
the next beach. Here, as the vista opened up in front
of her, Anna could see a party in full swing in the
sheltered sweep of the beach, just a short distance
away from the small harbour where a few boats
bobbed idly on the water.

Close by, at the foot of steps leading to a verdant,
terraced hillside, a barbecue had been lit, and the ap-
petising smell of food wafted on the air, teasing her
nostrils.

A couple of dozen people were dancing to the rip-
pling sound of steel drums on the wide sweep of sand.
Others were simply talking to each other as they
helped themselves to drinks from a selection of punch
bowls that were set up on a table in the shade of palm
trees. More tables were laden with a tempting array
of food—rice dishes, chicken, fish and salad, along
with every kind of fruit imaginable.

'My car's parked over by the quay,' Carlos murmured, leading the way and nodding to people he recognised as he passed by them. 'It's just a short drive
to the clinic.'

'Aren't you going to take him to the hospital in the
town?'

He shook his head. 'The Mount View Clinic is
nearer, and he'll be diagnosed more quickly there.'

'Oh, I see.' She frowned. She had heard of the
clinic. It was a private enterprise, where cardiac patients were treated mostly, but presumably there was
a range of other facilities, too. Carlos must be a man
of means, to be able to drop in there at a moment's
notice and still rely on getting immediate service.

They walked swiftly to the quay and found his car. It was impressive-looking, a large executive, midnight blue car. He settled Seb carefully into a child seat at the back, and the boy asked tentatively, 'My mama?'

Carlos bent down to him. 'Your mama was feeling a little poorly, Seb… Nothing bad, just that there was too much heat and it made her feel a bit faint. She has gone to lie down for a while. I'll make sure that you see her as soon as we get back from the clinic. Will that be all right?'

The boy hesitated a moment, then nodded. 'I fink so.'

'Good. That's settled, then.' Carlos came around the car and held the door open for Anna. She slid into the passenger seat and immediately felt the luxury of the car cloak her. Then Carlos climbed in beside her and started the engine, and they were on their way. They took the mountain road, following a circular route and climbing higher all the while.

They had been travelling for little more than five minutes when, as they swung around the next bend, the landscape suddenly opened up.

Anna caught her breath as she took in the sight of the wide sweep of a bay, with blue, crystal-clear waters reflecting the golden glitter of the evening sunlight. Above the bay, set back against the verdant mountain slopes, was a large, sand-coloured building surrounded by trees and exotic tropical plants.

That surely must be Mount View. It was the only building around and it was majestic, with wide windows and flower-filled balconies overlooking the sea.

It looked like a massive five-star hotel, Anna

thought as they approached it and finally drew to a halt on the wide driveway in front of the main doors.

'Here we are, Seb. Let's get you inside and take a picture of that shoulder. Then we'll be able to see just what's happened.'

Seb looked anxious, and Anna said gently, 'No one's going to do anything to hurt you, Seb. There's nothing at all to be worried about. I expect the doctor will give you something to take away the pain.'

Once again, Carlos picked up the child and took him into the building. Anna followed, her eyes growing large as she looked around the foyer. It was opulent in here, with deep-pile carpeting and smooth marbled pillars and overhead fans that hummed gently and made her think she was in another world. This was just a sample, and she could only imagine that the rest of the clinic was equally grand.

She daren't think how much it would cost someone to stay in a place like this. If the truth were known, she had never been comfortable with the fact that some people had to pay for treatment when they were unfortunate enough to be ill.

'We'll take him along to X-Ray first of all,' Carlos murmured. 'I'll have a word with the radiologist and explain the situation.'

'It's only a picture, Seb,' Anna explained. 'Just like having your photo taken, only the photo shows a little bit of what's inside you.'

Within minutes Seb had been X-rayed by a young woman who gently coaxed him into sitting for her. The boy looked wide-eyed and uncertain, and Anna smiled at him reassuringly.

Just a short time later the radiologist brought the films to Carlos.

'Look, you can see it quite clearly,' she murmured. 'They show a clean break.'

He looked at them carefully, then nodded. 'He'll need to keep the figure-of-eight bandage on for a while, until it heals.'

Anna was surprised at his confident statement. Did he know about medicine?

He hunkered down beside Seb and showed him the films. 'Can you see where the bone is broken, Seb?' He drew a long finger along the X-ray film. 'There it is, see? You'll have to take care not to knock it again. If you keep the bandage in place, it will mend and in a few weeks it will be stronger than ever.'

He smiled at the boy. 'Let's go and get you something to take the pain away. You've been a very brave boy. I'm proud of you.'

Seb managed a small smile, and held onto Anna's hand as they walked along a wide corridor.

It occurred to Anna that Carlos seemed to know his way around the place very well. He was leading them to the treatment room now, and his stride didn't falter once.

'That wasn't so bad, was it, Seb?' she asked as they walked along. 'We'll go and see the nurse now, and we'll ask her to put a dressing on the cut on your head as well as give you medicine.'

The child hadn't shown any signs of drowsiness or nausea so far, and she felt fairly confident that there was no concussion. She was glad of that. He had suffered enough and she didn't want to see him go through any more than he had already.

As a doctor, she ought to be able to keep a sense of perspective…a certain amount of distance between herself and the patient, she knew that…but it was much easier said than done. Somehow, each child she came across in her line of work managed to wind his or her way into her heart and steal a little bit of her…and Seb did remind her so much of her small nephew.

'Hello, Mr Barrantes.' A young, fair-haired nurse came to greet them and usher them inside the room. She looked down at Sebastian. 'What's happened here? Poor Seb, you look as if you've been having a bad time of it.'

Clearly, she knew Seb as well, and Anna found herself getting more and more puzzled as time went by.

'I felled over, and I broked my bone,' Seb told her. 'It hurts.'

'I bet it does, and you've banged your head, too. You poor little thing. Let me have a look at you and see if I can make you feel a bit better.'

Carlos lifted him up onto the treatment couch, and stood back a little as she gently dealt with the cut on the child's forehead.

As the nurse set to work, Anna said quietly to Carlos, 'People seem to know you around here. Seb, too. Are you frequent customers?' If they were, it didn't sound too good, did it? Were they always having accidents like this?

He made a wry face. 'They know me because I

own the clinic,' he told her. 'I'm a doctor, a surgeon. I work here.'

'Good heavens.' Anna was astonished. She blinked up at him, and tried to take it in. 'Now I see how you managed to find your way about the place so easily.'

Even so, she frowned. Just because he was a doctor and owned the clinic, it didn't alter the fact that the little boy had been allowed to wander off and get into that situation in the first place.

Surely someone in his position should have known better? He hadn't responded to her comments before, though, had he? Now, more than ever, she wanted to know what had happened.

CHAPTER TWO

KEEPING her voice low so that Seb and the nurse wouldn't hear, Anna said carefully, 'You still haven't explained to me how Seb managed to wander off on his own. As far as I understand it, his mother wasn't feeling well and he was left to his own devices, and that could have led to something very serious happening. He could have ended up being much more hurt than he was. I'd like to know what happened.'

Carlos studied her thoughtfully. 'His mother was taken ill quite suddenly...nothing serious, but she is pregnant and the heat made her feel faint. When she collapsed, we all rushed to help her, and I think Seb may have slipped away while we were making sure that she was all right.'

He glanced at the little boy, who was sitting up straight on the couch and beginning to appreciate being the centre of attention as the nurse fixed a dressing in place on his forehead.

'Perhaps he was frightened and wanted to get away from all the fuss. When I turned around to reassure him that his mother was going to be all right, I realised that he had gone and I went after him. I don't suppose he was out of our sight for more than a few minutes.'

'Oh, I see...' At last he had given her some kind of explanation. 'I suppose that's understandable, up to a point,' she conceded doubtfully. 'Children are like quicksilver, aren't they? They can be lost in a flash.'

'Unfortunately, you're right.'

The nurse said with a smile, 'All finished. Just a spoonful of medicine now.' She popped the spoon in Seb's mouth and he swallowed carefully. 'There. Good boy. We're all done.'

She smiled up at Carlos and handed him the bottle of painkilling medicine. 'You can take him home now.'

Carlos helped the child down from the couch and held his hand as they went back towards the car. Seb was walking proudly now, Anna noticed with a smile, showing off the sticker that the nurse had placed on his shirt.

On the drive back to the quay she said, 'Have you had the clinic for a long time?' Carlos looked too young to have achieved so much. He was probably only in his mid-thirties, and she couldn't imagine how he could have established something like that in just a short time.

'I had it built about four years ago. Mostly we treat cardiac patients there, although we sometimes carry out other treatments as well. For a long time I thought there was a need for a clinic out here. A lot of people want to be able to have cardiac surgery fairly quickly after they've been diagnosed as needing it. They don't want to run the risk of their condition deteriorating before an operation is available. Unfortunately, there was nowhere locally where they could go. The hospital waiting lists can be very long.'

'So you believe that you're fulfilling a need.'

'I'm sure that I am.'

'It must have taken a small fortune to establish something like that,' she murmured, 'let alone to keep it running.'

He didn't appear to be taken aback by the directness of her comments. 'That's true enough. I was fortunate. I inherited a certain amount from my grandparents, who used to be landowners, and, of course, there are sponsors who take an interest.'

It wasn't long before they arrived back at the harbour, and Carlos slotted the car smoothly into a parking place by the quay. Anna glanced at Seb and saw that he was falling into a slumber, his eyelids flickering faintly as he tried to keep them open.

She said softly, 'Look at him. He's tired out. It must be all the stress of the afternoon catching up with him.'

'I'll take him back to his mother so that he can rest,' he murmured, going around to lift him out of the car. Seb leaned his head on Carlos's shoulder and he looked so cosy that Anna guessed he would soon be fast asleep. 'Come and join the party on the beach for a while, and I'll come back to you in a moment.'

'There's no need for you to do that,' she said quickly, as they walked towards the shore. 'Stay with him. His mother might still be feeling ill and not able to look after him.'

'Someone's with her. I made a point of making sure that she wouldn't be left on her own. I have to come back here anyway and organise a few things. Stay a while and enjoy the food and have something to drink. You must be thirsty by now, and it's the least we can do to thank you for looking after Seb. I'm really very grateful to you for everything that you've done this afternoon.' A smile tugged at his mouth. 'Please, wait for me. I'll only be a minute or so.'

'Well, maybe just for a little while,' she told him. She *was* thirsty after the heat of the afternoon, and for the moment the sights and sounds of the Caribbean were all around her, helping her to relax. The food smelt delicious, and the gentle lilt of the music began to gradually work its way into her soul.

'I'll get José to look after you while I'm gone. If there's anything you want, just ask him and he'll get it for you.'

It was all done so smoothly. Carlos made a simple, quiet request, and his wishes were obeyed without hesitation.

José came over to her right away. He was a young man in his late twenties or thereabouts, lean and dark-haired, and he didn't seem to mind at all being asked to take care of her.

'Let me get you a selection from the table,' he said, disappearing for a few minutes and then coming back to hand her a plate that was piled high with delicious titbits to tempt her palate. 'I've brought you a glass of fruit punch, too. I think you'll like it,' he added with a wry grin.

Anna accepted the glass from him and took a careful sip of the drink, rolling it lightly over her tongue and feeling the instant kick in her throat as she swallowed.

'Rum?' she asked, her eyes watering, and he nodded, smiling.

He was right—it did taste very good. She tried to relax and enjoy what was left of the afternoon, sampling the food he had brought her with appreciation and occasionally taking a slow sip of her drink. After a few minutes she went to sit in the shade of the palm trees and watch the festivities going on all around her.

The people were friendly and quite a few stopped to chat, curious to know about the English girl in their midst. For the most part she answered amiably enough, saying that she was here to work and expected to stay for several months, but she carefully evaded any searching questions about her background.

Carlos Barrantes's friends, especially one or two of the younger men, wanted to know if she had any romantic attachments back home, but she wasn't about to give them any details of her love life. One young man, perhaps encouraged by a little too much alcohol, became slightly more amorous in his attentions than the others, but just as she was beginning to feel uncomfortable José appeared, and the man melted into the distance.

'Thanks,' she murmured gratefully, guessing that he had been keeping watch, and he nodded.

'Are you OK?'

'I'm fine, thanks.'

She wasn't sure she was ready to handle romantic overtures right now. Over the last year or two, she had come to the conclusion that romance simply didn't seem to be working out for her. Perhaps her ideals were set too high, but she felt a strong need to be cautious around men. She certainly didn't want to repeat the mistakes that Sarah, her sister, had made. Sarah's marriage had gone badly wrong, and now her husband, Nick, had taken their child.

At least now that Anna was out here she might be able to talk to Nick and persuade him to see Sarah's side of things. He couldn't just go off halfway across the world with their child and expect to get away with not taking him back home, could he? With all the miles that separated them, it was difficult for Sarah to sort things out herself.

Thinking back to that phone conversation with her sister just a few hours ago, she gave a shaky sigh.

'I'm sorry to put all this on to you, Anna,' Sarah had said huskily. 'I just don't know what else to do. I don't want to involve the authorities just yet, not while there's still a chance we can sort things out between us.'

'I think that's probably the best way to handle it for now,' Anna had told her. 'And you mustn't worry about me. I want to help any way I can, and it looks as though I'm going to be close enough to where Nick lives to be able to keep an eye on things. I'll let you know as soon as I find out anything at all, I promise.'

'It's so unfair,' Sarah had said. 'He was supposed to have brought Daniel back to me after four weeks, and there's been no explanation at all as to what's happened. I had a feeling he would do something like this. I hate being stuck here with this wretched broken leg and having to leave everything to you.'

'I know it's hard, but you must try not to worry,

Sarah. It will only wear you down. Anyway, it's not as if he's disappeared into thin air, is it? We'll find him soon enough, and I'll talk to Nick and have a go at making him see sense. I'll do whatever I can from this end, I promise.'

Anna took another sip of her drink, and mulled over the conversation. She rubbed her bare arms as a breeze stirred the trees around her and she felt suddenly chilled. Lost in thought, she wondered what had happened to the heat of the sun that had warmed her up until now. Clouds were beginning to build up across the blue of the sky, and it looked as though rain was threatening in the next hour or so.

A shadow loomed beside her, and Carlos Barrantes said, 'You're looking very solemn, Anna. *Lo siento.* I'm sorry…I hope I haven't kept you waiting for too long.'

She blinked, adjusting her gaze to take in his tall, powerfully muscled figure. 'No, it doesn't matter. You weren't gone for very long at all.' Absently she chafed her bare arms once more.

'Are you cold?' His gaze slanted over her slender curves, and she quickly shook her head.

'No, I'm fine.' His eyes narrowed as she made the denial, and to fend off any further enquiry she asked, 'Is Seb all right?'

'He's fast asleep.'

'I thought he might be.' She smiled. 'I suppose the medicine will have started to work.'

'I should imagine so, by now.' He glanced around, nodding to José, who appeared to be mouthing a question to him, and Anna watched the interchange, wondering what it was all about.

He turned back to her a moment later. 'I'm sorry about that… I didn't mean to be inattentive, but José needed to borrow my car.'

The music had stopped while they'd been talking, and it gradually began to dawn on Anna that something odd was going on all around them. There was a good deal of movement taking place as tables were cleared and the musical instruments were being packed away and carried off in some haste. It was plain to see that the party was breaking up, and people were beginning to leave.

She was puzzled. Why had the leisurely atmosphere suddenly disintegrated ever since Carlos had returned? True, the air was cooler now but, even so, it didn't seem reason enough to abandon the festivities so abruptly.

'Everyone appears to be leaving,' she murmured. 'I think maybe I had better go, too.' Perhaps she would head for the harbour and try to find Nick's house.

He frowned. 'It's not a good time to think of leaving just now, with the wind getting up. It happens here sometimes…not often, but the weather can change and it can become blustery very quickly.'

'I expect I'll manage,' she said. She looked around, and realised that the crowd of people was rapidly dwindling. It all seemed so strange. Why was everything happening so quickly? Was something going on that she didn't know about?

'Where did José have to go?' she asked uneasily.

'He's going to drive some of my friends home. It will be quicker for them by car.'

'You put a lot of trust in him, don't you?'

'Yes, I do. He works for me at the clinic, and I've always found him to be reliable.' He searched her face keenly. 'Didn't he look after you properly?'

'He looked after me very well.'

'Good,' he said. 'That's what I had expected.' He cast a careful glance up at the sky where dark rain-clouds were beginning to gather and murmured, 'We should talk later. Just now it's more important to think about your safety. I'm afraid we're in for a storm, and we should take shelter.'

'But the weather was beautiful just an hour or so ago,' she said in surprise. 'Surely it will pass?'

'I'm afraid it won't. Things can get out of hand quite quickly out here in the Caribbean, and I think we should be taking cover before it gets too bad. Let me take you up to my house where we can be comfortable.'

'Oh, no, you don't need to do that. I'm not afraid of a summer storm.'

His brows met in a dark line. 'I don't think you understand,' he said, his voice threaded with serious-ness. 'This is no summer squall. There has been a hurricane warning on the radio, and we have just a short time to prepare ourselves for what is to come. It is important that we find shelter as soon as we can.'

'A hurricane?' she echoed, the breath leaving her lungs in a sudden rush. 'I wasn't expecting anything like that so soon after arriving in the Caribbean.'

'There is no doubt, and this is the hurricane sea-son.' His gaze flicked over her. 'What matters now is that we get away from here as soon as possible.'

She shook her head, unable to take in what he was saying. If it was true, it really was bad news…but surely it wasn't very likely after a lovely day like today? As to going along with him, she really wasn't in any hurry to shut herself away with a man she had only just met, no matter how respectable he appeared to be. Anyway, surely his priorities should be his wife and his child?

'I can look after myself,' she said, crossing her fingers mentally that she would be able to get back across the bay before the wind took hold. 'It will only take me a few minutes to get home. I only live across Blue Water Bay—'

'No, that's too far. I really can't let you take that risk.' His expression was darkly autocratic now, his mouth held in a firm, unyielding line. 'I must insist that you come with me.'

'No…that's all right, I can manage.' She didn't know an awful lot about hurricanes, but from what she had heard there was usually time enough to get to safety and batten down the hatches.

She started to turn away, but he caught hold of her arm and brought her back to him.

'Since you're with me,' he remarked crisply, 'you're my responsibility. We'll stay together.'

'I can take care of myself,' she protested.

His mouth made a derisive twist. 'I don't think so. You have no idea what you are up against. You're obviously very new to this area, or you would understand what I am saying.'

He started to draw her away from the beach towards a flight of steps that led to higher ground.

She said quickly, 'Look, I have to get to the harbour. I need to meet up with someone.'

'I'm afraid your meeting will have to wait. Right now you have to come with me, and this is no time to argue.'

Carlos held her firmly, and his touch had such a potent effect on her nervous system that heat surged through her veins, pulsing like an electric current until her ears throbbed with sensation. She tried again to pull away from him, and he looked down at her in exasperation.

'We don't have time for this,' he said grittily. 'If you don't stop behaving like a foolhardy juvenile, I shall be forced to throw you over my shoulder and carry you up to the house. Believe me, that will not improve my temper.'

His features were determined, and Anna had no doubt he meant every word of it. Dry-mouthed, she shivered as an unexpected gust of wind swirled around her and buffeted her with such force that it threatened to topple her over.

Carlos reacted instinctively, his arm closing around her and pulling her into the shelter of his hard body, so that her soft curves were crushed against him. The breath caught in her throat as she registered taut male sinews and powerful muscles.

Around them, the once smooth beach was being stirred up into a mini-sandstorm, and pieces of driftwood that had lain on the beach just a moment ago were lifted as though by some invisible force to be

held aloft on a wild current of air. Seconds later they
were hurled in a willful paroxysm of violence against
the harbour wall.

She watched it all happen with a sense of shock. It
came to her then, in a heart-stopping moment, that
perhaps what he had been saying about the storm was
the truth after all, and the hurricane must be more
imminent than she had imagined.

The awful reality was that she was stranded here,
and totally dependent on him.

CHAPTER THREE

A TURBULENT blast of air eddied around Anna, whipping at her legs, so that she had to struggle to keep her filmy skirt in place. Holding onto it as best she could, she finally asked in a small voice, 'How long is the hurricane likely to last, do you know?'

He looked up at the brooding sky, then threw her a sideways glance. 'It's hard to say. It could be over by morning, I suppose.'

Anna's jaw dropped. *By morning?* There was no way she was prepared for that.

He must have seen her look of horror, because he said dryly, 'I see you've recognised the seriousness of the situation at last. Perhaps now we can hurry up and find shelter before we both become yesterday's news.'

A pulse started to hammer in her throat. She pulled in a shaky breath and tried to calm herself, desperately hoping that he couldn't hear or feel the sudden frantic thudding of her heartbeat. Around her the wind swirled and tormented, lifting her hair and tossing it about with reckless abandon.

Carlos wasn't about to wait for her to get herself together. 'This way,' he said, tugging on her arm and pressuring her towards the steps that led away from the beach. 'We've wasted enough time already.'

He moved so fast that she might have stumbled if

it hadn't been for him practically lifting her off her feet and hauling her along with him. They went swiftly towards the quay, then bypassed the harbour front and started to turn away from it towards higher ground. Here there were steps built into the hillside, and he took her up them, keeping hold of her as he balanced himself against the force of the wind with a hand firmly gripping the rail.

Anna began to tremble violently as the cold air assaulted her bare arms and legs, and she put up a hand to protect her face from the lash of the biting wind.

'Lean into me,' he said, drawing her up against his hard, masculine frame. 'Let my body shield you from the gale.'

He had her in a firm grip, crushing her to him so that their bodies meshed, and there was no room for her to manoeuvre. Her legs tangled with strong thighs and she could feel the vitality pulsing through every part of his body.

How could this be happening to her? She had only met this man just a few short hours ago and now here she was pressed up against him in a way that did nothing whatever to spare her blushes.

Her only consolation was that he was generating a good amount of heat to counteract the chill of her bare limbs, and that wasn't altogether surprising, given the amount of energy he was expending, battling with the elements. She relished the warmth that closed around her like a blanket, and tried not to think about the enforced intimacy.

'It's not far now,' he said, and she marvelled at his

stamina. Her own breath was coming in short bursts after all the exertion, yet his voice was as deep and firm as ever. 'My house is just a bit further up here.'

She was wholeheartedly glad that it wasn't far away. Around her she could hear the creaking of trees and the rattling of loose weatherboards on the houses, the slam of wood as it hit stone, and it was scary to think that all this chaos had erupted in such a short time. She was almost thankful that Carlos was so close, and that his male strength was something she could rely on.

They climbed for a few minutes more, then he led the way along a narrow, winding route until they came to a private road leading to a high stone wall. Halfway along the length of the wall there was a gated entrance, marked by pillars on either side.

'Here we are,' he said, aiming a remote-control device at the wrought-iron gates so that they swung slowly open. 'This is my home.'

By now the force of the wind was making breathing painful and the only way to avoid the brunt of it was to keep her head down. After they had hurried some way along the drive, though, Anna looked up, and then gasped as she saw in front of her a magnificent, white-painted plantation-style house.

It was two storeys high with a covered veranda all around, as far as she could see, and a corresponding upper balcony. Pale blue shutters sealed off the windows from the storm, and she wondered who had taken care of that task. His wife, probably. It must mean that she had recovered from her earlier bout of illness.

It would also mean that Sebastian was here and that she would most likely see him again. It would be good to see him when he was more like his normal self, after the initial pain of his injury had worn off.

Carlos let them into the house through the screen door, and as soon as they were inside the wide entrance hall, and the inner door was shut behind them, Anna became aware of the total contrast between this and the outside world.

While Carlos made a quick check of the alarm system she took the time to push her fingers through her long, wind-tousled hair, and then she looked around. The hall was as large as a room in itself, the floor laid with palely gleaming golden oak, and in all reflected a pleasing atmosphere of peace and serenity.

Her gaze was drawn to the finely textured wall coverings all around, which had a delicate, silk-like quality, soft hued to reflect the light. The high ceiling added to the impression of openness, and the flower arrangements that adorned little alcoves here and there added vibrancy and colour. The whole effect was welcoming and inviting, and she couldn't help feeling that in here they might be well and truly secure from the havoc being created outside.

She stood for a moment, simply absorbing the quiet of the place. Then it slowly began to dawn on her that perhaps there was another explanation for the apparent tranquillity. Could it be that the wind outside had dropped as suddenly as it had begun?

Carlos came to stand beside her and she asked tentatively, 'Is it my imagination, or have things suddenly quietened down?'

'They may have calmed for the moment,' he agreed. 'Though we'll feel it less in here anyway because of the high walls surrounding the place.' He threw her a cynical, narrowed glance. 'You weren't, by any chance, thinking that the storm might suddenly be over, and that you could actually leave, were you?'

She felt the betraying heat race along her cheekbones. Why did the man have to see right into her thoughts like that? She tried a nonchalant shrug. 'I just thought there was the possibility it might have blown itself out, that's all.'

'You don't know much about hurricanes, do you?' he said pithily.

Her shoulders stiffened at his tone. 'Not an awful lot, no.' She resented his sarcasm, and she tacked on succinctly, 'But, then, I haven't spent most of my life in this region of the world.'

'That's been fairly obvious from the outset,' he commented. 'Just to be absolutely clear about what's going on—this one may be in its infancy just now, and we may be experiencing a bit of a lull, but generally a hurricane will grow and become more powerful, and when the storm returns the wind will be back in full force. Believe me, you wouldn't like to be out there when that happens.'

She pulled in a quick breath at his clipped summary. 'I suppose I'll have to take your word for that, won't I?' This whole situation was making her edgy with frustration and she looked at him with doubt clouding her eyes. 'I'm new to all this,' she said raggedly. 'It isn't something I was prepared for.'

His eyes glinted. 'Is that a concession? Can I take it that you're resigned to sitting it out now?'

She winced. 'I don't appear to have any other options, do I?'

He raised his eyes heavenward. 'At last, she begins to see sense.' Moving closer, he placed a hand at her elbow and nudged her forward. 'Come on through to the living room, *por favor*. You'll be more comfortable in there.'

He drew her across the hall to another set of doors that opened out into a large room, bordered completely on two sides by full-length glass windows. These were blanked off right now by louvred shutters, which somehow cleverly managed to let in a degree of natural light.

Someone had lit the lamps that sat on tables or in little nooks, and golden light spilled out to enhance the warmth of pastel-toned walls. Had his wife done that, too? Had she gone to settle their little boy and soothe him while the storm lasted?

That thought gave her some degree of comfort as she stood for a moment, trying to take it all in.

'This is beautiful,' she said at last, softly, her glance travelling slowly around the room. She really hadn't expected to be so overwhelmed by the sheer elegance of this house, but it truly was beautiful, and there was a feeling of light and spaciousness in everything she had seen so far.

In here, all was simplicity, each item in the room flawless, from the delicately figured silk screen that stood to one side and the graceful simplicity of a Grecian statuette to the stylishly upholstered sofas that faced each other across the smooth lines of a low, glass-topped table.

He indicated the sofa nearest to her. 'Sit down, and I'll get you something to drink,' he suggested. She settled herself on one of the softly cushioned seats. 'Would you like coffee, or something stronger?'

'Coffee will be fine, thanks.'

He left her then, and she sat back and looked around once more, feeling the ravages of the last hour slowly ebb away. She wondered about Carlos, and about how much of the character of the man was revealed in this house. Everything in the room had been carefully chosen, she guessed, to reflect an exquisite taste, a desire for those fine touches that would add to the perfection of the architectural design.

When he came back a few minutes later with a tray of coffee, Anna said quietly, 'Have you lived here long? It looks as though you've put a lot of time and effort into making this house special.'

'This was my parents' home at one time,' he said. 'It's built on the edge of a coffee estate they owned for many years before they moved on to other projects. My father is more interested in the manufacturing side of things nowadays, food processing and so on. He's American, and he has a lot of interests in the United States, as well as here.'

He placed the tray on the table and she saw that he had laid it with coffee-pot, cups and a plate of freshly made triangular-shaped sandwiches, along with a selection of nibbles that looked enormously tempting.

'What about your mother? Does she have a career of her own?'

'She writes for magazines, mostly. Articles on the places that they visit or special cookery features. She's Spanish, so she tends to enjoy writing about dishes with a European flavour.'

'It sounds like interesting work,' Anna commented with a smile. 'So, what has happened to the coffee estate? Has it been sold?'

'No, I took it over from them.'

She frowned. 'Isn't that an awful lot of work for you with all your other commitments? The clinic, I mean.'

'It could be, but this estate is in partnership with several others, and I have managers to oversee it. My work as a surgeon takes up the bulk of my time.'

She was puzzled. 'What made you take up medicine when you had all this? You can't have needed to go in for all that training, all the hard work, when you could have simply carried on in your father's footsteps.'

'*Es verdad.* That's true enough…but I had a young friend who had a heart problem,' he said quietly. 'His family had travelled a lot, and he developed rheumatic fever when they were in a country where medicines were hard to come by. The fever damaged a valve in his heart.'

He frowned, thinking about it. 'I watched him struggle day by day. He couldn't even walk a short distance to the shops without becoming short of breath, and he was often in pain. More and more I found myself wishing that something could be done to help him. In the end, a surgeon replaced the valve in his heart, and after that his health was much better.'

She could imagine how he would feel. 'That must have had a profound effect on you.'

'It did. It made me think a lot about medicine, and when I went through school I became determined to study hard. Later on I decided that I wanted to take up surgery. Luckily I had the dexterity to manage it.'

'And then you set up your own clinic.' She smiled up at him. 'Do you still see your friend? He must be very proud of you.'

He nodded. 'You've met him already.'

'Have I?' She was puzzled, thinking back to all the people that she had met this afternoon.

'José looked after you, didn't he? He's been a friend of mine for a long time.'

She was startled. 'I didn't realise…he looks so well.' She frowned. 'What does he do at the clinic? Did he take up medicine as well? I wouldn't have thought he would be strong enough to face up to the rigours of training and all the hours on the wards. It's a very demanding job.'

'You're right. He chose to work in administration instead. He's very good at what he does.'

He pushed a plate towards her. 'Help yourself to a sandwich. It's getting close to supper time, and you must be hungry again by now.'

She glanced down at the slim gold watch on her wrist. 'Heavens…' she said with a faint sense of shock. 'I hadn't realised how fast the time had slipped by.'

'Does that matter?' he asked with a wry twist to his mouth. 'There isn't much you can do if you're

caught up in the middle of a hurricane except to sit
it out.'

She grimaced. 'I suppose you're right. I'm sorry
that I didn't take on board what you were saying
straight away. It just hadn't occurred to me that I
might be caught up in one almost as soon as I landed
here. It's really good of you to take care of me like
this.'

'You're very welcome. It's the least I could do, to
make sure that you're safe.' He made a face. 'These
storms happen on and off at this time of the year.
Mostly we're prepared for them, and on average
they're not on a grand scale so they don't wreak the
havoc you might expect. It's only every few years or
so that one comes along and is so fierce that it's given
a name of its own.'

'You're used to them, then?' She helped herself to
a sandwich and bit into it with appreciation, surprised
to discover that she was actually very hungry.

'You could say that.' He took a swallow of his
coffee and put his cup down. 'Why don't you tell me
about yourself? You said you had only just arrived
here. Does that mean you're here for a holiday?'

She shook her head. 'No, I'm not on holiday. I'm
here to work.'

'Really?' His tawny eyes flashed with interest.
'Tell me about it. What kind of work will you be
doing?'

'I'm a doctor, too,' she explained. 'I'll be working
at the public hospital, on the children's ward mainly.'

His dark brow lifted. 'That explains things,' he said
thoughtfully. 'I wondered how it was that you were

able to help Sebastian so well. At the time I thought perhaps you had learned first aid.' He smiled at her. 'So, are you a specialist…a paediatrician?'

'That's right. I've always wanted to work with children, as far back as I can remember, but I came to a point where I wanted to widen my experience.'

'Is that what you're going to be doing here?'

She nodded. 'I want to learn something more about tropical medicine, so when this job came up I thought it would be ideal. I've travelled quite a bit with my parents in the past—my father's a TV journalist and he reports from various parts of the world—but I've never visited the Caribbean until now. I thought this would be a great chance to get the best of both worlds.'

'Do you know anyone out here?'

'Only my brother-in-law. He lives by the harbour, and I was hoping to see him while I'm over here.'

'Perhaps I know him. What's his name?'

Was it likely that Carlos would know Nick? Then again, her brother-in-law was a wealthy man, too, and maybe his path had crossed Carlos's at some point. She said quietly, 'Nick Armand. He has a house close to the Harbour Lights Hotel.'

'Nick Armand, the hotelier?'

'That's right.' She gave him a searching look. 'Do you know him?'

He nodded. 'I do. He's a good friend of mine, as it happens. But you won't find him at home.'

Anna frowned. 'How can you be sure of that?'

'He's gone away for a few weeks with his young

son…your nephew, presumably. He had it in his mind to go on a tour of the islands.'

Anna gasped. 'Are you sure?'

'Don't you believe me?' Once more the brow lifted.

Anna winced.

'What I meant was that I just didn't expect him to have taken off like that with Daniel…not without say-, ing anything to anybody…to Sarah, I mean…to his wife.'

'His wife is in the UK,' he said laconically. 'It was her choice to stay there, from what I've heard. Nick is simply giving his son the kind of childhood he believes he deserves, a chance to have fun and see something of the world.'

'He doesn't have the right to just decide things like that on a whim, though, does he? Daniel should be with his mother.'

'Should he? Has that been settled in the courts? As I understand it, there has been no divorce as yet.'

Anna drew in a deep breath. 'I'm not going to discuss my sister's marital affairs with you. Daniel was supposed to be returned to his mother weeks ago! They had an agreement.'

His mouth made a cynical twist. 'It doesn't look to me as though that agreement stands any longer.'

Her green eyes sparked. 'You don't see anything wrong in what he's doing, do you?' Carlos was very much like Nick in a way, a wealthy man with all the authority and self-assurance that affluence brought. She guessed he would be used to having his own way in most things, and he would more than likely take Nick's side.

He shrugged eloquently. 'Who is to say that a mother is always the best parent for a child? Men can have an equal capacity to love their offspring. It isn't written in stone that a child should always be with his mother.'

'I've always believed that the bond was unbreakable,' she said in a strained voice.

'I'm not saying that it isn't. I'm merely pointing out that there are two sides to be considered.' His glance skimmed her taut features. 'When he gets back in a couple of weeks' time you'll have your chance to talk to him, and perhaps then you will have a more open mind on the situation.'

She shook her head. 'I shan't change my mind.' This wasn't good news, and it was difficult for her to accept that she would simply have to sit back and wait for Nick to return. Added to that, some time in the next few hours she would have to phone Sarah and break the news to her. It wasn't a conversation she was looking forward to.

'Let's not argue about it, anyway,' he said with a faint smile. 'You were telling me about your new job. I'm sure it must have been an opportunity too good to miss. How long will you be here for?'

'Several months. I'm here in place of someone who has taken maternity leave.'

She was distracted momentarily by the sound of the wind howling through trees outside, whipping at the branches until she heard ominous cracking sounds. So Carlos had been right, and the gale was back. Fearfully, she wondered what kind of devastation was going on all around them. It was almost too frightening to contemplate.

'Don't think about the storm,' he told her, and she looked up with a start to see that he had been watching her. 'You're safe enough from it in here. The walls are strong and the shutters are all in place to protect the glass. Believe me, this place has stood the test of time, and there's nothing that can be damaged in even the severest gale.'

She chewed at her lip. 'Yes, I can see that must be right. It's just that it takes some getting used to.'

'Try to forget about it. You were telling me that you're here for a few months,' he prompted her, and she wondered if he was trying to take her mind off things. 'What happens after that?'

With an effort Anna dragged her attention back to what she had been saying. 'I suppose after that I'll have to take some time to think about what I want to do. There was some talk of a job in London being made available for me. At least I'll have gained greater knowledge of tropical medicine and, the way I see it, the more experienced I am in all forms of medicine, the more choices I'll have in the long run.'

He helped himself to a sandwich. 'That sounds sensible enough.'

She nodded. 'And in the meantime, I thought I would make the most of being here in the Caribbean. There's no point in coming somewhere like this and not seeing as much of it as you can. I've been reading up on some of the best places to visit. If I get the chance, I'll try to fit some of them in whenever I have time off.'

'You don't want to stick to the tourists'' favourite haunts,' he said wryly. 'There are other beauty spots—quiet, secluded places that are less well known to the cruise-ship passengers.'

'I expect you have to be a local to find them.'

'True enough.' His glance flicked over her. 'I could show you, if you like.'

The offer had come out of the blue, and now she eyed him cautiously. Perhaps he thought she had been hinting.

'Thanks…' she murmured. 'That's very kind of you, but I expect you'll be too busy with other things to do that.' She needed to tread warily here, didn't she? After all, why would he want to spend time with her, when he had a wife and child who were relying on him to take care of them?

'Other things?' he queried lightly.

'Well…your family, for a start,' she answered on an even note. 'I'm sure they must expect you to spend your free time with them.' How uncaring could he be, that he needed her to spell it out for him? 'Especially your son. After all, he's not much more than a baby, and he needs you.'

He threw her an odd glance, but recovered his composure soon enough, looking at her in a strangely detached way so that for a second or two she thought she might have struck home. Then, bemusedly, he repeated, 'My son?'

'Sebastian. Don't you think he depends on you?'

He blinked, clearly needing a moment to take this

in. Then he said softly, 'Ah…now I think I see what's going on in your mind.' He paused before adding, 'There is one thing I should perhaps tell you…'

'What's that?'

His gold-flecked gaze rested on her upturned face, his mouth shaping a faint smile. 'I am not Sebastian's father.'

She let out a small gasp. 'But…but he called you Dada Carlos…'

He seemed to be amused by that. 'He has called me that ever since he has been able to talk. His father is away on business quite a lot, you see, and his mother—my sister—has relied on me to act as a father figure in many ways.' He gave a rueful grimace. 'Unfortunately, I think the name has stuck.'

'Oh…' Anna didn't know what to say.

'Oh, indeed.' His tawny eyes sparkled as he registered the pink flush of her cheeks.

Dazedly, she tried to take it all in. How could she have got things so wrong? Everything that had happened this afternoon and evening seemed to have conspired to confuse her, leaving her uneasy and uncertain.

She sent him a troubled glance. 'Then…you're not married,' she managed weakly, still trying to adjust to everything he had said.

'I'm not married.' His lean, sculpted features seemed to darken a fraction, a muscle flicking along the line of his jaw.

She said weakly, 'And you don't have a child?'

His brows drew together. 'That goes without saying.'

It also explained how the house could stay looking so perfect, didn't it? Everything she had seen so far was immaculate, not a thing out of place, and it simply didn't look like the sort of home where a child could rampage about.

She drew in a deep breath. 'I had expected that Seb and his mother would be here. I thought, when I saw that the lamps were lit and the shutters were drawn, that someone must have prepared the place. I assumed it must have been your wife…'

He shook his head. 'Martha, my housekeeper, would have done that before she went to her own home. She's very good, and the truth is I rely on her far more than I should. She has never let me down.'

'Oh, I see.' She was floundering now. 'Somehow, I had taken it for granted that I would see Sebastian again. I was sort of hoping that I would see him when he was fully recovered.'

His mouth made a crooked shape. 'Somewhere along the way you've developed a soft spot for him, haven't you?' His glance shifted lightly over her guarded expression, then he said wryly, 'You're much too sensitive to make a good doctor, Anna. How on earth will you cope with the children on your ward if you worry over each one with such intensity? You'll end up as a shadow, with all the substance drained out of you.'

'I'd sooner that than not to care at all,' she retorted stiffly.

His sceptical glance spoke volumes. As though to underline her difficulties, she heard the shutters begin to rattle, as though the elements of nature were building up to a crescendo of rage once more and were making a determined effort to shake them loose. She hoped Carlos had been right when he'd said they wouldn't succeed.

'Why don't you try to relax?' he suggested, reading her strained expression.

Anna wasn't too sure that was possible. After all, she was alone in the house with a man she had met only that afternoon, and from the furious sound of the storm outside she was likely to be with him for some time to come. Added to that, she had discovered that there was no wife and no child to act as a protective barrier.

He was watching her, waiting for a response, and she said carefully, 'Maybe I'll feel happier when the storm is over.'

'Possibly.'

She wasn't fooling him for a moment, and she found herself wondering if it was possible that he could actually read her mind.

He reached for the coffee-pot. 'Would you like more coffee?'

She shook her head. 'No, thanks. I've had plenty.' She stretched, trying to ease limbs that were beginning to ache after the climb up from the harbour. 'Actually, I'm feeling quite tired now. Perhaps I ought to go and freshen up. That might make me feel a bit better.'

'I'll show you where the bathroom is.' He got to his feet and said lightly, 'If you want to call it a night now, that's fine by me. The storm isn't going to let up for a few hours yet, so you may as well settle yourself to the idea of staying over. You can have my sister's room, if you like. She uses it when she comes to stay, so there are clothes of hers in there that you can borrow.'

'Won't she mind?'

'It's highly unlikely. Saskia's very laid back and, anyway, at the moment she wouldn't fit into any of them.' A gleam lurked in the depths of his eyes. 'She's about seven months pregnant and showing every bit of it.'

'Will she be all right? You said she was feeling faint earlier, didn't you?'

'We have to keep an eye on her. She was anaemic, so her obstetrician prescribed iron tablets, but until they take effect she's tired a lot of the time. Then her blood sugar varies, so that's another thing that needs watching.' He grimaced. 'The biggest problem is that the baby's lying in an oblique position. It will mean that we have to take special care during the delivery, because if it doesn't turn before then she'll need a Caesarean section.'

'Presumably the decision to go ahead with that will be taken in good time. It's not something her doctor would want to leave to the last minute.'

'Try telling my sister that. She hates the thought of an operation.'

He waited while Anna stood up, then led the way out of the lounge and up a flight of stairs. At the far end of the landing he pushed open a door and said, 'Here we are. This is Saskia's room.'

Like the rest of the house, it was furnished in exquisite taste. The divan bed looked soft and inviting to Anna's weary eyes, and she fell in love with the sun-drenched colour scheme, reflected in the warm apricot bedcovers and the filmy voile curtains that were draped across floor-to-ceiling windows.

Carlos crossed the room and drew back a sliding glass door. 'Your bathroom's through here. Help yourself to whatever you need, and if you can't find what you want, just ask.'

She followed him, her gaze travelling over the ivory-coloured suite and gleaming gold fittings, and the glass shelving that housed all manner of toiletries. She would be spoiled for choice. There were ornaments, too, dainty porcelain swans and little dishes filled with an assortment of bath pearls and perfumed soaps, which added a delightful touch to what was already a beautifully feminine room.

'Oh, it's lovely. Thank you. I shall be fine in here.'

Anna turned to him, a smile curving her mouth, and then she caught sight of a mirrored wall to one side of the room. Lifting her glance, she let out a little cry of dismay as her reflection stared back at her.

'Oh, no…oh, how did that happen? I look an absolute fright…'

The woman in the mirror looked like a total stranger to her, an untamed, wanton creature with a mass of honey gold curls tumbling about her face and shoulders in wild disarray, her green eyes wide and startled. As to her clothes…she daren't even think about the state they were in. The fabric of her skirt had moulded itself to her thighs, leaving even more of her legs bare than before. As to the top, it must surely have shrunk.

'Oh, lord,' she muttered. 'I didn't realise…'

Carlos looked on with lazy interest, his glance moving warmly over her from head to toe as he leaned negligently against the wall.

'You look absolutely fine to me,' he murmured, an odd huskiness coming into his voice. 'Slightly tousled maybe, a touch abandoned…but very definitely sexy.'

His gaze lingered momentarily on her softly feminine curves, a smile touching his mouth. 'And a body that would turn hearts to flame,' he added thickly. 'But it's the eyes that add the finishing touch, I think… Pure emerald…beautiful.' His mouth tilted. '*Madre de Dios*…if I were a saint, I'd relinquish my vows of chastity here and now.'

He moved away from the wall, coming closer, and Anna flashed him a warning glance. 'Don't even think about it,' she muttered.

He laughed softly, making a wall with his hands in self-defence. 'It's OK,' he murmured. 'I got the message.'

'Good,' she said huskily. 'I'm glad about that.' She looked at him warily, her emotions totally confused.

With a rueful twist to his mouth, Carlos started to ease back from her. 'I'm going,' he said.

Anna watched him walk away, but he paused at the door, turning to say softly, 'Of course, if you should change your mind at any time…' A half-smile played over his lips. 'If the storm should bother you, for instance…'

'I won't change my mind,' she told him cautiously, and waited for him to go.

Obligingly, he stepped out of the room, closing the door behind him, but the unmistakable rumble of his husky laughter stayed with her, drifting mockingly on the air.

CHAPTER FOUR

ANNA blinked as sunlight streamed in through the windows and made a feathery dance on her eyelids. Still dazed from sleep, she stared around her, taking in every angle of the unfamiliar room until at last she remembered where she was. Carlos's house.

She sat up in bed and looked quickly around. Someone must have come in and pulled back the shutters while she slept, because there was sunshine and warmth in every part of the room, the start of a beautiful new day.

There was no sign of Carlos, but there was a tray with a pot of freshly made tea on the table beside the bed and a silk robe had been carefully laid on a chair by the dresser.

She frowned. How long had she slept? Was it very late? One thing was for sure, she had better get a move on and get herself washed and dressed before he had the chance to walk back in and throw her into confusion all over again. A flush of heat suffused her whole body as she thought back to last night and the way he had looked at her.

The clothes she had worn yesterday had mysteriously disappeared, so she had little option but to search the wardrobe and borrow something of Saskia's as he had suggested. A cool-looking pale yellow shift dress looked about the right size, and she slipped it on, thankful that it fitted her as though it had been made for her, except for the length which was a little shorter than she would normally have worn. She would tell Saskia how grateful she was if ever she had the chance to meet up with her.

Hurrying downstairs a few minutes later, she went looking for Carlos, and heard noises coming from a room somewhere to her left. It was probably the kitchen, judging from the clatter of pans, and she headed in that direction.

A buxom woman was standing by the hob, skilfully tossing eggs in a pan, but she turned when she heard Anna come into the room.

'Hello, there.' The woman greeted her with a smile. 'I'm Martha. Sit yourself down at the table, girl. I've cooked you some eggs.' She scooped the mixture from the pan and slid it on to a plate.

Anna returned the smile. 'That's how I like them. Thank you.'

'Good. You go on, then, and get started.' She nodded towards the oval table. 'Best you eat 'em while they're hot.'

Anna sat down at the table, and did as she was told. The food was delicious, and there was a jug of hot coffee to wake her up to the day. She helped herself and wondered where Carlos was, but when she asked the housekeeper, she simply shrugged and said, 'He had to go out. He's always busy, busy.' She rolled her eyes heavenward. 'He works too hard. Even on Sunday, he has to go out. He says you must wait for him to come back, please.'

Anna wasn't too sure about that. Who could tell

how long he might be? She still had a lot to do in preparation for work tomorrow. 'Was it you who brought me the tea and opened the shutters in my room?' she asked.

The woman nodded. 'It's good to see the sun in the morning. My old bones don't like the cold.' She gave a mock shiver. 'Last night was no good at all.'

Anna finished breakfast a few minutes later, and when Carlos still hadn't come home she decided that she couldn't wait around for him. Perhaps the hurricane had affected the plantation in some way and he would be delayed for some time.

'Thanks for breakfast,' she told Martha. 'I'd better be on my way now. I'll see to it that Saskia's clothes are washed and sent back just as soon as I can.'

'But you are going to wait, aren't you, girl? Lord, what will Mr Carlos say when he gets back, if you've gone already?'

'I'm sure he won't mind at all, Martha. I'll leave him a note to thank him for letting me stay, and I'll explain that there are things I must do. I really can't stay any longer.'

Her first day at the hospital started bright and early.

'So you're Dr Somerville?' Tom Raynor, the registrar, greeted her with a smile and clasped her hand warmly in his. He was tall and slim, young for a registrar, Anna guessed, perhaps in his early thirties, with fair hair that was tidily cropped. 'I'm glad to meet you, Anna. I've heard a lot about you, and I'm happy to have you on board. From what I've heard, your qualifications are quite impressive.'

'Well, thank you,' Anna murmured. 'I'm looking forward to working here.'

'You might not be so keen after you've been here a while,' he said with a laugh. He drew her towards the office. 'Have you had a chance to look around yet?'

She shook her head. 'Not yet. I had to come in on the bus this morning, and it didn't leave me much time.' With all that had gone on over the weekend, she hadn't managed to sort out a car for herself yet. The bus had dropped her off outside the gates, and that was the first sight she'd had of the hospital.

It was a modern building, large by any standards, with separate blocks for Outpatients, Pathology and Clinical Sciences. The wards were housed in wings that looked out onto paved and attractively land-scaped areas.

'Well, not to worry. Come and have a coffee, and then I'll show you around before the morning rush starts. We've been really busy here just lately, so your input will be more than welcome. You'll be covering all the main paediatric wards along with me—surgi-cal, medical and infectious diseases—but we'll start you off on admissions this morning.'

The morning rush came before they were ready. There were two admissions in the first hour, both pa-tients with fractures, and Anna hardly had time to take a breath before a third child was brought in.

She hurried forward, ready to assess the child's condition, then came to a sudden halt when she real-ised with a shock that the man carrying the infant was Carlos. He was dressed in formal clothes this morning, and she had a swift impression of an expensively tailored grey business suit and a beautifully laundered linen shirt. Even his shoes looked impeccable.

'*Buenos dias*, Anna,' he murmured, slanting her a quick glance. 'I have a small patient for you. Her name is Jessie. Will you attend to her, *por favor*?'

Anna's mouth had dropped open in surprise at the way he had appeared out of the blue, and now, as he quietly voiced his request, she clamped it shut and tried to pull herself together.

'Of course.' The nursing team quickly found a trolley bed and Carlos gently laid the infant down on it.

The dark-skinned little girl was just a baby, really, Anna judged, about eighteen months old, and she looked very poorly. She was listless, and there was a bluish tinge about her mouth. Then she coughed and squirmed in distress, breathing raggedly.

Anna bent over the child. 'Hello, chick,' she said softly. 'Poor little one…you're not very happy today, are you? Let's have a look at you and see what's wrong.'

Very gently, she examined the child, soothing her as she listened to her chest through her stethoscope. There were bubbling noises coming from the tiny lungs, and she was wheezing. Anna checked her temperature. When she had finished, she looked up and saw a young woman hovering anxiously nearby.

'Are you Jessie's mother?' she asked.

The woman nodded. She, too, was dark-skinned, probably in her early twenties, tall and slender, and she was beautiful, with well-defined cheekbones and a full, wide mouth.

Carlos intervened smoothly. 'Anna, this is Grace, Martha's daughter.'

Anna was startled. 'Really? Hello, Grace.' She smiled at her. 'I've met your mother. She was very kind to me.' She paused for a moment, then asked, 'Can you tell me how long Jessie has been ill?'

The child coughed again and began to cry miserably, and Grace looked at her distractedly, biting her lip.

'She's been snuffling these last few days,' she said. 'I thought she just had a cold, but this morning she was hot, and she doesn't look right.' She was shaking her head, clearly fretting about the little girl. 'I asked Mr Carlos if he would have a look at her. I don't like asking but I don't know what to do.'

Carlos shook his head. 'That's all right, Grace. You did the right thing.'

Anna said quietly, 'I think it was a good thing that you brought her here. I believe that Jessie has a virus infection which has affected her lungs and made her feverish. She's finding it quite hard to breathe just now, and I think she needs a little bit of help to make her more comfortable.'

Grace looked anxious. 'What will you have to do?'

'We can give her oxygen and humidify the air for her so that she won't have to struggle so much. We'll arrange for her to have physiotherapy as well to help clear the mucus from her chest.'

Grace's eyes widened. 'She needs to stay here?'

'Yes, I think so, Grace. She'll be better off in hospital for a few days at least, until her chest is clear.'

The mother said shakily, 'It's bad, then? Is she very

poorly?' The child coughed again and started to cry, and Grace reached down to stroke the infant's hair with a trembling hand.

'She is poorly, but this is a virus that can some-times affect children of Jessie's age,' Anna said gently. 'It isn't unusual. She'll be better off in hos-pital, you know…we can keep an eye on her here.'

Grace was looking deeply unhappy, and Carlos in-tervened softly, 'You could stay with her. I'm sure we can find you a place to sleep. It won't be anything grand, but at least you'll be close by. Would you like to do that?'

Grace nodded, and he gave her a slight smile. 'We'll arrange things for you.'

Anna said quietly, 'It will be reassuring for Jessie to have you close by. We'll move her onto the ward now, and we can start the treatment straight away. I'll prescribe a course of antibiotics to prevent any sec-ondary bacterial infection. Try not to worry. You can rely on us…we'll take very good care of her.'

The nurse on duty came to take them both up to the ward, and Anna wrote out the treatment chart, then said, 'Maria will look after you both. If there's anything at all that you're bothered about, just ask away.'

Carlos reached out and touched Grace's arm. 'I'll come and find you and see how you're doing. If there's anything you need, just let me know.'

'Thank you. Thank you for seeing Jessie and for bringing us here.'

'That's all right. You're welcome.'

The nurse took Grace and the child away, and in

the quiet that followed their departure Anna looked around and realised that she was now alone in the examination room with Carlos.

She glanced up at him. 'We'll look after her.'

'I know you will.'

She said hesitantly, 'I'm sorry that I couldn't stay yesterday to say goodbye to you. There was so much I had to do back at the apartment.'

'That's all right. I understand. Did Martha look after you all right?'

'Yes, she did, thanks. I didn't know how much longer you were likely to be. I wondered if perhaps your crops had been affected by the storm and that might be the reason you were delayed.'

'No, it wasn't that. My crops were fine. The beans had already been harvested and sent for processing. I was called out to the clinic, and things took longer than I expected.' He grimaced. 'It came at a bad time… I'd hoped to drive you home, and make sure you were all right.'

'It didn't matter. Anyway, your patients come first.' She shrugged lightly. 'I'm all right, as you can see.'

Perhaps the shrug was a mistake. His glance followed the movement, slanting over the skirt and top that clung to her like a second skin. Then his gaze lifted to dwell on her shining, freshly washed hair, and she saw a faint glint of amusement come into his eyes.

'I certainly can.'

A flush of heat ran through her cheeks. She didn't need three guesses to know what he was thinking, did she? The memory of that night would haunt her for ever, and no matter how conservatively she dressed from now on, that wanton image would always be with her. As to her hair, it still refused to be tamed, but at least today she could be confident that it was clean and lustrous with health.

She said cautiously, 'I imagine Martha must be worried about her little grandchild. It must have seemed as though Jessie's illness came out of the blue.'

'She was concerned about her,' he said, and there was compassion in his voice. 'That's how I found out about it—she told me that she thought the baby was feverish, and there was something about all this that didn't sound quite right. I didn't think it was just a cold, so I decided I'd better go over to Grace's house and see for myself.'

'It's just as well that you did.' She looked at him with warmth in her eyes. 'She could have been very ill if she'd been left much longer.'

'I know. Just as I know you'll look after her now that she's here.'

'You can depend on it.'

He smiled at her, then glanced down at the watch on his wrist. 'I should go or I'll be late for my ward round. It's supposed to start in five minutes and I don't want to keep my patients waiting any longer than I have to. I'll see you later, Anna.'

He turned and moved swiftly away, and for the second time that morning Anna felt her jaw drop.

'Ward round?' she echoed, but he was already striding out of the room and within moments he was moving briskly along the corridor. She swallowed hard and started to go after him, but instead she had a breathless collision with Tom Raynor at the door. He had been carrying some books and files, and now they all dropped to the floor.

'Whoah,' he said, laughing. 'Slow down. What's the rush?'

She stared at him blankly, her mind still fogged by what Carlos had said. Then she looked at the books scattered all over the floor and bent to help him pick them up. 'I'm sorry, I wasn't looking where I was going.'

Absently, she glanced down at the files that littered the floor. 'What is all this?' she asked. 'Have I messed up anything important?'

'I'm studying for more exams,' he explained. 'I want to make consultant some day, so I'm working hard in my spare time.'

Fleetingly she scanned the covers of the textbooks as she handed them back to him. 'I'm impressed,' she said. 'You must have been busy raiding the library shelves for all these.'

'Only in part. Mr Barrantes lent me some.' He winced as he looked over the creased pages. 'With strict instructions to get them back to him in good condition.'

'Oh, dear.' She grimaced, then moistened her lips with the tip of her tongue. 'Tell me about him,' she said in a strained voice. 'Does he work here?'

'Didn't you know?' Tom got to his feet and raked a hand through his hair. 'He's the visiting cardiac consultant. He's a brilliant man, one of the best surgeons in the field. He divides his time between several of the hospitals in the Caribbean, and we're lucky to have him around.' He looked at her closely. 'Why do you ask? Is something wrong?'

'Oh, no,' she said weakly, her head going into a spin. 'Nothing at all.' She straightened up. She had told the hospital's best cardiac consultant that he shouldn't have allowed a three-year-old to wander off on his own, and she had argued with him over parental rights. How would she ever live it down if that ended up on the hospital grapevine?

'He looked as though he was in a hurry when he swept out of here just now,' Tom remarked. 'Was everything all right?

She was beginning to recover a little from the shock, and she answered carefully, 'Yes, I think so. He was worried about being late for a ward round.' She paused, then said hesitantly, 'You obviously get along well with him, if he's lending you books. What's he like to work with?'

Tom looked thoughtful. 'He's OK, on the whole. Fair-minded, but he likes things done a certain way and he doesn't tolerate mistakes lightly. He can be a bit volatile occasionally, I suppose, but not usually without cause. Actually, he's been a bit preoccupied these last few months.'

'Why is that? Has something happened? A family problem?'

He shrugged. 'I'm not too sure. He's a very private man…but rumour has it that he was thinking of getting married to a girl he'd known since childhood, and then something went wrong. No one really knows what happened, except that she went away for a time.

It isn't something he talks about, and no one is going to volunteer to get their head bitten off by asking.'

Anna slowly absorbed that snippet of information. 'This happened recently, did it?'

He shook his head. 'No, all that happened a long time ago…but I do know that the woman came back recently, and they seem to be fairly close again. Her family has something to do with the Friends of the Hospital charity. The Marchants are very well-to-do, and Francesca's been around quite a lot lately to organise events.'

'Oh, I see,' Anna said flatly, then frowned. Why did she feel so deflated by what he had told her? She wasn't becoming attracted to Carlos, was she?

Tom interrupted her errant thoughts. 'You said you came on the bus this morning. Whereabouts are you staying? Maybe I could give you a lift home later?'

'That's a nice thought.' She smiled up at him. 'I'm leasing an apartment on Blue Water Bay. Is that on your way?'

'It certainly is. I'll come and pick you up at the end of the shift.'

'Thanks, Tom.'

He left a few minutes later, and Anna was called away to the examination room to assess a new patient. He was a boy in his early teens who had been brought into hospital by his parents.

The boy looked seriously debilitated, she thought, as well as thoroughly fatigued and sickly.

'We're on holiday,' the father told her. 'We came down here from Florida and we've been doing a tour of the islands. Jack hasn't been himself for about three or four weeks now, but we didn't think it was anything too bad to begin with. Then he seemed to go downhill pretty fast.'

Anna looked at her young patient. 'Perhaps I could examine you, Jack. Just lie back and relax while I check you over. Can you tell me how it started?'

'I was sick…vomiting,' he said, 'and then I started to ache all over.'

'A bit like flu?'

'Yeah, that's right.'

'We thought it was just something he'd eaten,' his mother put in, 'and we expected that he would be all right in a few days. He's been tired, and he hasn't wanted to eat, but we thought that was normal.'

Anna quickly completed her examination and noted that the whites of the boy's eyes had turned yellow, and that there was a similar tinge to his skin.

'I'll need to do a blood test to confirm it,' she told them, 'but I think what's happened is that Jack has a form of hepatitis. He's jaundiced, which means that his liver's not working properly, and that's why he feels so sick. It's not too serious, but it will make him feel ill for a few weeks.'

She wrote out the blood-test form and waited until the nurse, Maria, had finished settling the boy back against his pillows before handing it to her.

'We'll keep him here for a few days, just to keep an eye on him and assess him for treatment, but after that it's really a question of bed rest and special attention to his diet.'

'But he's hardly eating anything as it is,' his mother said anxiously.

Anna nodded. 'That's understandable. He won't be able to tolerate fatty foods while his liver function is disturbed, so we have to make sure that he avoids those for the time being. It's best if he has small portions of whatever he does eat in the meantime. When the time comes, we'll make sure that you have a diet sheet to take home with you.'

'Thank you, Doctor.' Jack's father looked doubtful. 'Will you be giving him some medication to help him over this?'

'Depending on the results of the tests, we'll probably give him steroids to help improve the liver function and analgesics to relieve his pain. Basically, though, this is a viral infection, and his system has to try to overcome the virus. The best way to help him to do that is to make sure he has plenty of bed rest and small but regular meals. I'm hopeful that in a few weeks' time he'll be feeling much better.'

It wasn't encouraging news to give them, but so far Western medicine hadn't come up with anything better. Hepatitis was a nasty illness.

Towards the end of her shift, Anna went to check on her smaller charges, making her way up to the ward where little Jessie had been admitted. She came across Carlos heading in the same direction, and they took the lift together.

'I thought I might find you on your way up here,' he murmured, glancing at her. 'Have you finished for the day?'

She nodded. 'I wanted to see how Jessie was before I go home.'

'How have things gone for you on your first day?'

'It's been hectic,' she said with a faint smile. 'To be honest, I haven't had time to think about how it was going…it just went. The time seems to have flown by.'

'Do you think you're going to be happy here?'

She nodded. 'I think so. So far, everyone has been really friendly and helpful. They see me looking lost and point me in the right direction.'

'They're a good bunch of people.' He flicked her a sideways glance as they stepped out of the lift. 'How are you getting home this evening? Do you need a lift?'

'I've got one, thanks. Tom's taking me…he said it's on his way.'

She didn't hear his murmured comment. He pushed open the door to the ward, letting her go through first, and she quickly scanned the room, looking for Grace.

They found her sitting by her daughter's bed. She looked up as they approached and made an attempt at a smile.

'How is she doing?' Anna asked quietly, picking up the infant's chart and checking her progress. 'Her temperature seems to have dropped a little. Is she breathing any better?'

'She's still restless,' Grace said, 'but I think she's sleeping.'

Carlos looked at the child, who was lying in a cot. 'Did the physiotherapist come and work on her chest?'

'Yes. She came a couple of hours ago.'

'It'll take time to clear her lungs,' Anna said, draw-

ing up a chair, and trying to reassure Grace. 'Her
colour has improved a little, I think.'

She sat down and scanned the woman's drawn features, noting the fatigue around her eyes. 'Are you all
right here? Have they found you somewhere to sleep
for the night?'

'There's a room I can use, just down the corridor.
But I shall stay here for now. I want to be here if she
wakes up.'

'As long as you don't tire yourself out. Have you
managed to get yourself something to eat and drink?
There's a cafeteria down on the next floor.'

'Yes, thank you. The nurse showed me where to
go. I'll be fine.'

'That's good. Try not to worry.'

'These are early days yet,' Carlos said, then
glanced obliquely at Tom, who had come onto the
ward and was approaching the bed.

Tom nodded to both of them, then turned to Anna.
'Maria told me you were up here,' he murmured. 'I
came to see if you were about ready to sign off for
the day.'

'Yes, I'm all done for now.' Turning to Grace, she
said, 'I'll be back on duty in the morning, but if
there's anything you're not sure about in the meantime, the nurses will help you out.'

'OK. Thanks.'

Anna got to her feet and took a last look at Jessie
before she started to leave the ward. She glanced at
Carlos. 'Are you heading home now?'

He shook his head. 'I'll stay and talk to Grace for
a while.'

She nodded and turned to walk away with Tom.

'I'll have you home in no time at all,' he murmured. He pushed open the swing door to the corridor and laid a hand lightly on her shoulder to usher her through.

'That's great. Thanks.' She looked up at him in appreciation, then glanced back towards Grace to give her a final wave, but it was Carlos's unreadable gaze that held her attention. He stirred up all kinds of odd feelings inside her, and she had absolutely no idea how to deal with them.

CHAPTER FIVE

SEVERAL days had passed, and Anna was at last beginning to relax a little. She was gradually becoming much more used to the general routine of the hospital, and at the same time she was quickly getting to know and like her young patients.

Jack, the boy with hepatitis, was still looking tired and drained, but she was pleased with his progress so far.

'You haven't vomited in the last two days, have you, Jack?' she asked now.

'No, I haven't. I hate being sick.' He opened his mouth and pointed a finger down his throat in a parody. 'Yeuk.'

'Yeuk's the word.' She chuckled. 'How are you feeling, apart from that?'

'Fed up,' he said, wrinkling his nose. 'I was supposed to be going to see the coral reefs and snorkelling, and instead of that I've been stuck in here, feeling rotten. It's not fair.'

'It isn't fair, that's true, but maybe you'll be able to do those things soon enough. The reefs aren't going anywhere.'

'Nor am I, by the looks of it,' he said in disgust. He started to scratch at his arm as he spoke, and Anna frowned, watching him.

'Is that giving you a problem?'

72

'It's an itch,' he said, rubbing even more vigorously. 'It's driving me round the twist.'

Anna took a closer look at the arm. 'It's part of the illness,' she told him. 'Sometimes your skin can get over-dry and that can be a bit of a nuisance. It might help to take a cool bath, but I can give you a lotion to relieve it.' She smiled at him. 'In the meantime, if you're nice to Maria she might find you a different computer game or something else to cheer you up and take your mind off things.'

His eyes brightened. 'A football game?'

'I expect we've got one somewhere. Don't play it for too long, mind. We don't want you tiring yourself out.'

She made a note on his treatment chart and handed it to Maria, leaving the pair of them to chat as her pager started to bleep. At least the boy was feeling well enough to complain. Checking the pager, she went over to the surgical ward, where the staff nurse met her at the door.

'Would you come and have a look at Joseph for me?' Suzy Monterey was a conscientious girl, slim and dark-haired and looking a little anxious at the moment. 'His blood pressure's rising and I'm concerned about him.'

'He's one of Mr Barrantes patients, isn't he?' Anna asked.

'Yes. Mr Barrantes operated on him yesterday morning. He'll be in to see him later today, and I don't want to call him before time if I can avoid it.'

'I don't suppose he would mind if you were worried about one of his patients. Even just a phone call would be enough perhaps, then he could decide for himself whether he needed to come in.'

'Oh, I did phone him, about an hour ago. A woman answered, though—Marchant, I think she said her name was—and she said he'd had a very late night and had only just gone into the shower, so it wasn't a good time to call him out unless it was an emergency. I wasn't sure I could class this as an emergency.'

'I see.' Anna swallowed hard. Was this the same woman that Tom had told her about, the one Carlos had been planning to marry at one time? It had to be, didn't it? And from the sound of things…if she had stayed there the night…she was definitely back in his life. Why else would she be there when he had only just got out of bed?

Anna's mind closed down, a cloak moving in on her imagination. For some reason she didn't want to think about why he'd had a late night.

'Have I done the wrong thing in asking you to come and look at him? I waited a while, but I was beginning to get more concerned about the boy.'

The girl's anxious question brought Anna abruptly back to the problem at hand. 'No, of course not,' she said quickly. 'You did absolutely the right thing. Call me at any time if you're concerned. I don't mind at all.' She made an effort to focus. 'Mr Barrantes operated, you said. Did the surgery go all right?'

'Oh, yes, there were no problems at all. Mr Barrantes is very good, everyone says so. It's just that I'm fairly new around here, and I don't want to make any mistakes, especially where Mr Barrantes is concerned.' She added nervously, 'He's very particular about his patients. Everything has to be done just right.'

Anna could understand her wariness if she was new to the hospital, though her caution was probably misplaced. 'OK, don't worry. I'll go and have a look at him and try to find out what's happening. Are his parents around?'

'They've gone down to the cafeteria to get something to drink. Joseph was dozing, so they thought they would go together.'

Anna went over to the boy's bedside and looked down at him. He was just seven years old, she noted from his chart, a dark-haired, frail-looking boy who had a heart condition that had been present from birth. He stirred as she approached, and blinked up at her.

'Hello, Joseph,' she said with a smile. 'How are you feeling today?' His complexion, which she guessed would normally be olive, was pale, and there were dark shadows around his eyes. 'Are you in any pain?'

'No,' he mumbled, turning his head into the pillow. 'The nurse gave me something to take away the pain.'

'That's good.' Joseph didn't volunteer any more information, and Anna guessed that he was still weak from the surgery he had undergone.

She glanced down at his notes. He had been born with a defect that caused an obstruction to the flow of blood through the aorta, the main artery of the heart. Throughout his young life the pressure within the heart would have been high and its workload would have been too great to handle for any sustained length of time. The condition was quite rare, but if it was discovered, the optimum time for surgery was around his age.

'Is there a problem?' The deep voice intruded on her thoughts, and she looked up in surprise to see Carlos standing by her side. Her glance tracked the length of his tall, powerfully masculine figure, and her pulse began a chaotic thump-thump before she quickly brought herself under control.

'His blood pressure is raised,' she explained. 'We weren't expecting you in until later, so Suzy asked me to check him out.'

'I decided to come in early so that I could take a look at him.' He nodded to Suzy, and said quietly, 'You did the right thing in getting an opinion. Better to check up than leave anything to chance this soon after an operation.'

Had Francesca passed on the message after all? Anna's mind swerved away from that tricky area, and she tried to concentrate on the job in hand. She was familiar with the surgery that Carlos had carried out. He would have removed the section of the aorta that was obstructed, and then he would have carefully rejoined the two ends so that the blood could flow without restriction. Even so, there could often still be a problem with high blood pressure after surgery.

He went over to the bedside and looked down at the child. 'Are you feeling sleepy?' he asked the boy softly, and Joseph nodded. 'That's OK,' Carlos murmured. 'I won't disturb you for long. I just want to have a quick look at your chest to make sure that everything's all right.'

The child was too lethargic to make any comment so Carlos gently went ahead and examined the site of the incision. Anna could see that it was perfectly clean and that there was no sign of inflammation.

'That's looking fine,' he told the boy, tucking the sheet carefully back in place when he had finished. 'Try to get some rest now. I'll come and see you again a bit later on.' He went to join Suzy at the nurses' table in the middle of the ward.

Anna glanced at Joseph's bedside table and saw that there was an action figure toy lying on its side. 'Is this your soldier friend?' she asked, and the boy nodded soberly.

'He's been fighting,' he whispered.

'I thought he had. He's wearing a bandage, isn't he? Do you know, I think he might feel better if he lies down next to you. Would you like that?'

The boy nodded, and Anna put the figure carefully into his hand. She was rewarded with the glimmer of a smile.

As she walked back to the others, she was conscious of Carlos's gaze resting steadily on her. By the time she reached them, though, he was saying quietly to Suzy, 'I think for the time being we'll increase the dosage of the blood-pressure tablets. That should bring it down a little. Once the wound settles down internally, we may be able to lower it again. The diuretics should help with that.'

'I'll see to it,' Suzy said.

He looked at her directly. 'You did the right thing in calling me this morning. It doesn't matter if I'm not due in. I always want to be kept informed.'

Suzy was smiling with relief as she went to see to the medication, leaving Anna alone with Carlos.

'Are you going to be free for lunch today?' he asked, and she was so startled that she found herself nodding.

'I think so, unless something crops up in the meantime. I was going to the cafeteria at about one o'clock. Why?'

'Something I wanted to ask you…it'll wait till then. Good. I'll see you later. I need to go and check up on another of my patients now.' He gave her a brief smile and went off in a bit of a hurry, leaving her to wonder what on earth he could want to ask her. Still thinking about it, Anna returned to her own work.

She spent the rest of the morning in Casualty, dealing with a crop of accidents mostly involving tourists. One was a teenager who had been brought into hospital by his parents.

'This is Toby,' the young nurse said, drawing back a curtain in the treatment room. 'He thinks he might have been bitten by something.'

Toby barely looked up as Anna went into the examination cubicle. He looked to be around thirteen years old. He was sitting morosely on the couch, staring at the floor as though he resented being dragged in here when he could have been doing more interesting things.

'I'd better have a look at you, Toby,' Anna said cheerfully. 'What do you think might have bitten you?'

He managed a brief glance in her direction and pulled a face. 'Dunno.'

Thankfully his father had a little more to say on the subject, and with a look of exasperation he told Anna, 'He was swimming in the lake by our campsite a few days ago. I told him it didn't look too clean and to keep away from it, but you know what kids are. Anyway, now he's got a rash on his leg. Maybe something had a nip at him when he was in the water. Or maybe it was a mosquito. I don't want him going down with malaria or anything like that.'

Anna picked up a magnifying glass and examined the inflamed area carefully, before saying, 'He won't suffer from malaria, you'll be glad to know…but, judging from what you've told me and from the rash, he might have been attacked by a little worm.' She put down the magnifying glass and looked at father and son.

'A worm?' They both echoed the word, and father and son were staring at her with horrified expressions.

'That's right. The larvae burrow into the skin and cause what we call ''swimmer's itch'' before it goes on to lay eggs inside the body. So what we have to do is give Toby a drug that will kill the parasite.'

'Ugh!' Toby bent double, looking as though he was about to throw up, and Anna smiled.

'It's not that bad, Toby. I believe we've caught it in time. If you'd delayed, you might have developed a very nasty illness called schistosomiasis, but you're lucky that your father brought you here right away. If I were you, I'd listen to him next time he tells you not to swim in infected water.'

'Oh, yipes…that's gross.'

Toby was still exclaiming some minutes later as his father led him away to the pharmacy.

'He thinks that's bad news,' a familiar, gravelly voice said, and Anna turned around, still smiling, to come face to face with Carlos. There was a gleam of amusement in his golden eyes.

She managed to say lightly, 'He wasn't too happy, was he?'

He lifted a dark brow. 'It's a good thing you didn't tell him the local story about how the little worm can battle his way upstream against the strongest current…and what might happen if he were to urinate in the water just as the little worm was swimming by…'

'Ouch! That doesn't bear thinking about.' She laughed, and Carlos's mouth crooked attractively. She found herself mesmerised by the slightest of movements of his face, watching the angle of his jaw, the way the corners of his eyes crinkled when he smiled.

'Are you about ready to go for lunch?' he asked. His gaze steadied on her, and she made a hasty effort to get a grip on reality. He was a consultant, he lived in another world from her, and it would be madness to let herself get carried away by daydreams, wouldn't it?

'Just about,' she murmured. 'Just give me a minute to sort my notes.' She signed a batch of treatment charts and handed them to the nurse, then added, 'I don't suppose there's any change in Joseph's condition? I was concerned about him earlier on. He didn't look too good, did he?' She couldn't help thinking about the little boy with the dark eyes who had been too weak to care much about what was going on around him.

'His system is still adjusting to the shock of the operation. He's never been a strong boy, but these are early days yet, and we'll do what we can to encourage his recovery.'

They walked together towards the cafeteria, and Carlos's gaze flicked over her. 'It was good of you to take the time to come and help out. You seem to have settled in here well. Is everything going all right?'

'Well enough, I think. At least I'm managing to find my way about the place now. I'm having to divide my time between several areas, but I think I'm getting to grips with it.'

'From what I've seen, you're coping brilliantly. You were very good with little Jessie, and Grace tells me you've made a point of going to see her every day. Last time I looked in on her, she was looking much better. I wouldn't have known she was the same child if I hadn't seen for myself how poorly she was to begin with.'

'Jessie improved by leaps and bounds once her lungs were clear. I'm thinking I might be able to discharge her soon.'

He nodded. 'I guessed you might. Grace was out of her mind with worry just a few days ago, but she's a lot more relaxed now. You helped both of them. Martha's happier, too. She was very concerned about her little granddaughter.'

'I'm not surprised. She was so tiny, and she looked helpless.'

'You look after all of your small patients very well.

Are you coping with the tropical medicine side of things? You said you wanted to gain more experience on that score—is it working out?' He pushed open the door of the cafeteria, and they went over to the buffet bar to make a selection from the food set out there.

'So far. At least, I haven't come across anything I can't handle yet...and Tom has been a great help.'

Carlos frowned, his brows drawing together in a dark line. 'He may not always be on duty at the same time as you. You shouldn't rely solely on Tom Raynor.'

'I won't, of course.' She wondered why he had reacted so sharply to that, but she guessed he was a stickler for having everything done properly. 'I have done my homework,' she murmured. 'I've been working towards this specialisation for some time, and I've been reading up on all the latest developments.'

He looked at her quizzically. 'That won't necessarily mean you won't come across something that has you flummoxed.'

She was thoughtful for a moment as she tipped pizza and peppers on to her plate. 'Actually,' she conceded, 'there was one incident that threw me. A woman brought a child in with a gaping wound, and when I took off the temporary dressing she had put on it, I was staggered to find that she had draped slices of pawpaw over the cut.' She had been startled to see the melon-like fruit used that way.

His eyes crinkled. 'That's not unusual hereabouts. People often bandage pawpaw in place and leave it for a couple of days. They believe it keeps the wound clean and helps the healing process.'

There was an empty table by the window, and they took their trays over to it.

'Does it work?'

'A lot of folk medicine works. Sometimes people cook pawpaw and eat one or two slices to lower a high blood pressure. They use coconut oil for scalp problems, and that seems to do the trick. They say it can be rubbed into the head as a cold remedy, too, but I can't say I'm too sure about that one.'

She grimaced. 'I've heard that honey is supposed to be a pretty good antiseptic, but I don't think I'd be too keen to spread it on a wound.'

His mouth twitched. 'You're obviously a modern-day woman. It wouldn't do for you to be stranded on a desert island and left to your own devices, would it?'

'Not unless someone was there to provide me with a fully packed medical kit and emergency supplies.'

His tawny eyes flashed, his glance travelling over her and searing her where it touched. 'In that case, I've no doubt you would have any number of men queuing up to help out,' he observed dryly.

His comment left her floundering. 'I don't know about that,' she muttered, her skin heating at his mockery.

He chuckled, then went on to say calmly, 'I want to ask something of you, *por favor*, to do with my small patient, Joseph.'

Immediately she sobered. 'Anything... Is something wrong?'

'Nothing's wrong, but his parents want him to be moved to the Mount View clinic so that he can convalesce there and receive more dedicated attention. He'll need to be supervised on his journey, and I wondered if you would agree to go along with him? I saw how you were with him today, and I'm sure he would be happier if you were there to keep him company. He's been asking for the golden-haired doctor who looked after his soldier friend.'

A smile touched her lips. 'Has he? I'd be glad to help any way I can. When is he going?'

'His parents want him to go there tomorrow evening.'

Anna frowned. 'Isn't that too soon?'

'Not if we take great care to see that his journey is smooth, and if you're there with him to watch his progress.' He looked at her thoughtfully. 'Did you have other plans for the evening?'

'Not exactly.' She hesitated, then went on, 'I had thought about going back down to the harbour to see if I can find Nick at home, but I suppose I could go today instead. I have to stay a little later at the hospital tonight, that's all, so I won't have as much time with them as I'd like. You did say that Nick should be back by now, didn't you?'

'That's right. That's one of the things I wanted to see you about. I heard from your brother-in-law this morning. They arrived home yesterday.'

'Did they?' Anna sat up, alert all at once. 'Did he mention my little nephew?'

'He said that Daniel had a great time on their trip.'

'It would be lovely to see him soon,' she murmured

wistfully. She thought about Sarah back home, counting the days.

'You're very fond of him, aren't you?'

'Oh, yes. He's my one and only nephew and I think the world of him.'

'Well, you'll probably be able to see him now.'

'I hope so. I'd like to be able to tell his mother that he's all right, and it would be good if he could just talk to her on the phone. Up to now, Nick has been awkward about keeping in contact, and I really want to persuade him that it's in Daniel's interests to be able to talk to his mother.'

He looked at her thoughtfully. 'Perhaps I should wish you luck?'

'Even though you don't see my side of the argument?' She pulled a face. 'To be honest, I think Sarah could do with a little luck.'

'If your sister is so concerned about her son, why hasn't she come over to see him? She must know where Nick lives.'

'It isn't as simple as that. She would have come, but she was knocked over by a joy-rider, and now she has a leg in plaster. Even so, she would have followed him, but her doctor wants to keep an eye on the injury. It wasn't healing as fast as it should.'

Carlos grimaced. 'I've always thought that joy-riding was a dreadful way to describe what actual happens.'

He paused, his glance narrowing on her. 'Does this mean that you'll be free go with Joseph?'

'Yes, I'll be glad to.'

'Thanks. I'll arrange for an ambulance to make the

journey to Mount View, and I'll bring you back here afterwards so that you can collect your car.'

She shook her head. 'You don't need to do that. I haven't managed to get one yet. With the hours I've been working here, there hasn't been time for me to sort anything out.'

'That must be tiresome for you. How have you been managing—do you get the bus?'

'No. It hasn't been too bad so far. Tom has been picking me up and dropping me off at home each night.'

'Has he?' His glance flicked over her. 'That's very good of him. I didn't think his shifts would always coincide with yours.'

'He said it wasn't any trouble, and that it was on his way.'

'Are you still looking to buy a car?'

'Eventually, yes, when I can get to a garage.'

He felt in his jacket pocket and brought out his wallet. 'I've a friend who is a car dealer,' he said, fetching out a card and handing it to her. 'Give him a ring and tell him that I recommended him to you, and he'll have a car delivered to your door. Just tell him the sort of thing that you want, and he'll arrange it. He won't overcharge you, and you can be sure that the vehicle will be sound. If you're not happy with what he brings, he'll take it back again at a later date.'

It sounded like the answer to her prayers. 'Thanks,' she murmured. 'Perhaps I'll do that.'

That evening, Anna went over to the harbour, hoping that she would be able to see Nick and little Daniel.

It would be good to be able to phone Sarah and tell her that she had made some headway.

As far as she could tell from the address Sarah had given her, Nick's home was close to the hotel that he owned, set back in its own grounds a short distance from the quay. She followed the path through the lush tropical gardens that bordered the hotel, breathing in the scent of exotic blooms, and came upon the white-painted colonial-style house just a few minutes later.

She went up to the pillared porch and rang the bell. Then she stood back and waited, trying to calm her breathing. She didn't want to be flustered, but so much depended on her getting this right.

Nick answered the door a minute or so later. 'Anna…' He frowned, then stepped back to allow her inside. 'Sarah told me that you would be coming out here. She said something about a job.'

'I'm working at the hospital,' she told him. 'I'm not living too far away from you either. I've an apartment in Blue Water Bay.' She looked around as he led her through the house, but there was no sign of Daniel.

'If you were hoping to see Daniel, he's already in bed and fast asleep,' Nick commented. 'I'd sooner not wake him.'

Anna tried not to be dismayed by his cool tone. She had only just made contact with him, and things were almost bound to be difficult at first.

'I can understand that,' she said softly. 'Do you think I could go up and have a look at him, though? It's been a while since I saw him.'

He looked as though he would have liked to have

refused, but he said grudgingly, 'Maybe just a peek, then. I don't want him disturbed. He's been a bit feverish lately, and he needs to rest.'

'Is he ill?' Anna was concerned. 'Is it anything serious?'

'No, he'll be fine. He just needs his sleep.'

She nodded. 'I'll be quiet. I won't wake him.'

He led her to Daniel's room, and she crept in and stood by the bed, looking down at the sleeping child. He had his thumb in his mouth and he was mumbling incoherently, little snatches of words that Anna strained to hear. He looked so small and defenceless that she wished she could pick him up and cuddle him and kiss his soft cheek.

Nick touched her arm, though, and signalled to her to go with him back down the stairs, and she realised with aching clarity that he didn't trust her. He was too guarded around his son, and she would need to tread very carefully.

As Carlos had said it would be, the ambulance was waiting when she finished her shift at the end of the following day. Seven-year-old Joseph had been transferred into it. He was still weak, but he managed a tentative smile when she went to sit beside him and she saw that he had not one but two action figures with him this time.

'Are they fighting each other?' she asked, but he shook his head.

'They're friends. Samson's helping Tank to get better.'

'He's looking better already,' Anna said thoughtfully. 'I expect he'll be able to have his bandage off before long.'

Joseph's parents were following behind in their car, since there wasn't much room in the ambulance, and Carlos had gone on ahead of all of them so as to be ready to shepherd his patient into the clinic.

Anna talked quietly to the boy as they drove smoothly along, but after a while he appeared tired so she let him rest and gazed out of the window instead, following their route along the winding mountain road.

'We're nearly there,' she told Joseph quietly a few minutes later. 'It's a beautiful place. I think you're going to like it there.'

The ambulance turned into a side road that led towards the building, and finally came to a halt in the parking bay.

Porters came to ferry the boy carefully inside, and his parents were already at the main doors, waiting anxiously to see that he had come to no harm.

Carlos gestured to Anna to come over, and she went to stand by the boy's trolley as his parents moved to one side.

'We'll take him up to his room and see that he's comfortable for the evening,' he murmured.

'OK.'

He led the way to the lift, and together they went up to the second floor. Here they disembarked onto a wide corridor, where paintings of Caribbean landscapes, orange groves and busy market scenes added bright touches of colour to the walls.

'Through here,' Carlos said, and the porters ma-

noeuvred the trolley into a large room where glass
doors opened out onto a balcony.

'Oh, this is lovely,' Joseph's mother said. 'It's so
clean and fresh, and you have your own television
and music centre. See?' A slight woman, with dark
curls framing her face, she smiled at Joseph and went
around the room, pointing out everything that would
brighten his stay. 'Your father and I have a room next
to this one, and there's a day room where you can go
to be with other children. This will be good,
Joseph…yes?'

Joseph smiled, but leaned back against his pillows,
and Anna said quietly, 'It's a lot for him to take in
just now. Perhaps we should take a few moments to
examine him and see that he's settled in properly.'
She glanced at Carlos, and he nodded, gesturing for
her to go ahead.

She took the boy's pulse and checked his blood
pressure, and found that both were slightly elevated.
'We should let him rest for now,' she murmured. 'The
move has been rather too much excitement for one
day, and he needs to sleep now. Perhaps later, when
he's more up to it, he'll want to look around.'

'You're right,' his mother said. 'We'll go and un-
pack our things next door, and look in on him later.'
She went to her son and kissed him tenderly. 'Close
your eyes and try to sleep and get well, Joseph. If you
need us at all, just press the buzzer, here, see?' She
handed him the intercom that linked his room with
theirs. 'We'll be back in a little while to see you.'

'A nurse will stay with you, Joseph,' Carlos said
gently. 'Her name is Freya, and she's going to look

after you while you're here. When you feel up to it, later on, she'll find you some toys to play with.'

He spoke quietly, aware that Joseph's eyes were already closing, and as Freya came forward to check his chart, Carlos went with Anna to the door.

'He's very frail,' Anna said softly as they walked back to the lift. 'What are his chances of a full recovery?'

'Only time will tell us that. With any luck, now that he has had the operation, we can start to build up his strength. At the moment he isn't eating very much, and that is one of the first obstacles we have to overcome.'

They took the lift back down to the foyer, and Carlos ushered her through wide double doors into a spacious room.

'I'll get you a coffee,' he said, 'and something to eat. Wait here, while I go and organise something.'

'Are you sure you have time for that? I know you have things to do with Joseph, and his parents will want to talk to you. I don't want to get in the way. I'm happy enough to sit and wait for you while you do that.'

He looked down at her, a smile tugging at his mouth, and he reached for her, his hands circling her arms. 'It's the least I can do to thank you for your help, Anna. It'll be more comfortable for you in here…it's more private, and you'll be able to relax while you're waiting for me.'

His touch was warm and gentle, and it made her feel incredibly secure and wanted. 'Thanks,' she said lightly. 'I hadn't expected you to take care of me like this.'

'*De nada*,' he murmured, dropping a swift and unexpected kiss onto her startled mouth. 'You're very welcome.'

The kiss stayed with her long after he had left the room. Her lips tingled in response to the feather-like brush of his mouth on hers, and she was bemused and bewildered by the whole experience. Why had he done that?

Anna touched her mouth with her fingers, savouring the sweetness of the memory that lingered there, until she heard sounds of movement in the corridor outside. How could she explain her dream-like state to anyone who might happen to come in here?

She looked around dazedly. The room she was in was furnished as a lounge, with inviting armchairs and low tables, and two walls were taken up with sliding glass doors. Confused, and needing to sort out her chaotic emotions, Anna went and opened the doors and stepped out onto the paved terrace, breathing in the scent of the sea air and the fragrant blossoms all around.

Carlos had kissed her, and now the blood was fizzing through her veins. She would never be the same again.

CHAPTER SIX

ANNA stared out over the terrace, looking at the beautifully landscaped gardens. In the distance, surrounded by shrubbery and a raised rock garden, there was a pond with a fountain, each droplet of water glittering in the evening sunlight.

'Hello…' A woman's voice sounded huskily behind her just a moment or two later. 'You must be Anna. Carlos told me that I'd find you in here.'

She turned to see that a young woman had come into the room. Her resemblance to Carlos was striking in the angular lines of her face, the straight nose and the beautifully shaped mouth. Her eyes were hazel, gleaming and alert, and her long, dark hair was cut in a feathery shape that enhanced her features. She was also very pregnant.

'You must be Saskia,' Anna said in surprise.

'I am. I am so very pleased to meet you, Anna. I've been wanting to thank you for the way you looked after Sebastian when I was taken ill.'

'I was glad to help. Are you feeling all right now?'

'Yes, thank you. I'm under strict instructions to put my feet up every afternoon, but you know how it is…' She laughed. 'There is always so much to do.'

'I can imagine. You must have your work cut out, looking after Sebastian.'

'That's true. For the moment, at least, he is with

Carlos, trying to cadge chocolate biscuits from him.' Her smile lit up her face. 'Carlos is very good with him but, then, he likes children. He has always got on well with young people.'

'Was he expecting you to come here today?' Anna couldn't get her head round the fact that Saskia was actually here, at the clinic. Was that a coincidence, or what?

Saskia nodded. 'Yes. He told me he would be here this evening, so it would be a good time for me to come over, and it fitted in with my plans. He took a blood sample from me just a moment ago to check my iron levels. He sometimes checks my glucose levels, too—they've been raised since I've been pregnant. It's easier for him to do it here, than it is for me to go to see my obstetrician.'

'I can imagine it would be.' Saskia was seven months pregnant, and right now she was looking slightly out of breath. Anna said gently, 'Shall we go in and sit down? I don't know how long Carlos will be, but you look as though you could do with getting the weight off your feet.'

Saskia chuckled. 'You're right. I'm totally worn out with chasing after Sebastian all day.'

Carlos came into the lounge just then, pushing a heavily laden tea-trolley. 'I keep telling her to rest more,' he said, sliding the trolley into position against the wall. 'She could take time out when Seb's at pre-school classes, but she never does. She's always busy doing something. I might as well talk to myself for all the notice she takes of me.'

Sebastian came from behind Carlos just then to

sneak one of the biscuits from a plate. Anna watched him, a smile touching her lips. He looked bubbly and full of fun, and it was a delight to see him like that.

'H'llo, Anna,' the little boy said through a mouthful of crumbs. 'See, my arm is much better now.'

'So I can see.' The arm was still in a sling, but he moved it almost freely and Anna said happily, 'I'm very pleased about that, Seb. I wondered how you were doing.'

Carlos came over to her and offered her a plate piled high with delicacies—spicy-looking patties, creamy hors d'oeuvres and cheesy nibbles. She selected a patty, taking a bite and savouring the taste on her tongue.

'Can I see the pond?' Seb asked, rushing over to the glass doors.

Saskia sighed. 'See what I mean? He's never still, this one.'

'I'll take him to look at it,' Carlos said. 'You two relax and get to know each other for a while.'

'Are there fish?' Sebastian wanted to know, and Carlos nodded.

'Yes. Lots of them. Come on, I'll show you.'

He took the boy out onto the terrace, and they walked out into the landscaped grounds, leaving the two women to help themselves from the trolley and chat.

When he came back a while later, Seb was full of what he had seen, and raced to tell Saskia. 'I nearly felled in,' he confided. 'I wanted to poke the fish with my finger, but Dada Carlos said, no, they wouldn't like that.'

Saskia raised her eyes heavenwards and Carlos chuckled. 'I held onto him,' he said. 'I know this little one. He's such a bundle of energy that you need eyes in the back of your head.'

Turning to Anna, he added, 'If you're ready, perhaps we should make a final check on Joseph, and then I'll see you back to your apartment.'

'Yes, I'm ready.'

'*Bueno.*' He glanced at Saskia. 'Who is driving you home? Do you want me to ask José to take you?'

'He has already offered. I just need to go and find him.'

Anna intervened. 'Why don't you both go and sort out your arrangements with José while I go and check on Joseph?' She smiled at Saskia. 'It was really good meeting you, Saskia.'

'Me, too. I expect I shall see you at your hospital barbecue in a couple of weeks, shan't I?'

'Barbecue?' Anna was puzzled. 'What barbecue?'

'Didn't you know?' Saskia's brow rose. 'Oh, you must go to it…everybody does. The Friends of the Hospital organise it…my brother is on the committee, so it will be very good…they try to raise funds. You will be there, won't you? It'll be fun. I shall really look forward to it if I know you'll be there.'

'Well…yes, if I'm not working, I expect I shall.' Now she came to think of it, over the last few days there had been murmurs about an event coming up, but she had been too busy to dwell on them at the time. 'I'd like to see you again, and Seb, too.' She bent down to Sebastian and ruffled his hair lightly. 'It was lovely, you being here. You take care of that arm, young man.'

'I will.'

When she had said all her goodbyes, she left them to go and sort out Saskia's lift home, and made her way up to Joseph's room.

The child was fast asleep. He looked peaceful enough now, though the shadows were still there around his eyes and his skin had an almost translucent quality about it.

Freya had been taking regular observations on his condition, and Anna was pleased to discover that his blood pressure had come down a little. Carefully, so as not to disturb him, she started to check his various tubes and drips for herself, and she had just about finished when Carlos came into the room.

'He's doing all right so far,' she murmured. 'I don't think the journey has upset him too much.'

He nodded, then looked at the sleeping boy and said in a low voice, 'Dr Sanchez will take care of him while we are off duty. He'll be in good hands. Come on, I'll take you home.'

The car ate up the miles with incredible ease. Carlos drove fast but with expertise, his hands in firm control of the wheel along the winding mountain road. They didn't talk much on the journey back, and Carlos switched on the CD player so that soft music filtered through the speakers. Anna leaned back against the richly upholstered seats and tried to relax.

It was difficult, though, with Carlos being so close. She only had to turn her head a fraction and she could see his long legs. The slightest movement strained the material of his trousers, accentuating the line of his powerful thighs.

She didn't want to be so aware of him, but just lately it had been getting to be more and more of a problem whenever he was near. He had his own very special kind of magnetism, but she had to work with him on an almost daily basis, and the last thing she needed was to have the blood rushing to her head whenever she set eyes on him. She averted her gaze, and concentrated on the view from the window instead.

It wasn't long before they had turned off the road that hugged the mountain terraces and turned instead onto the main route, which led into town.

'We're almost at the turning for Blue Water Bay,' he murmured. 'You'll have to show me which apartment block is yours.'

Now that they were getting closer to her home, Anna wasn't sure she wanted him to see where she lived. There were too many differences in their lifestyles, and this was just one more that showed how great the divide was between them. He was a wealthy consultant, the owner of a luxurious private clinic, and she was just a lowly junior paediatrician, living in a run-down apartment. The chasm that lay between them would be even more apparent when he dropped her off there.

'You could let me out here if it's easier for you,' she said when they reached the turn-off on the harbour road that led to his estate. 'I can walk the rest of the way.'

Cool eyes surveyed her briefly. 'I'll take you to your door.'

There was nothing for it but to go along with him. She just hoped he wouldn't be too taken aback by the place she called home for the time being. It wasn't situated in the best part of town, and in her building as many apartments as possible had been crammed into a small space. The corridors were poky, and the walls were so thin that you could sometimes hear what was going on next door.

Its saving grace was that her living room looked out over Blue Water Bay, and every time she sat at the window and took in the beautiful view, she felt at peace with herself. She didn't think Carlos would be impressed, though. It wasn't at all what he was used to.

'This is it,' she said at last, reluctantly. 'This is where I live.'

He parked on the road outside the main entrance, and came around to the passenger side of the car to help her out and walk her to the front of the apartment building.

It was quiet at this time of the evening. Most of the families who lived here would be indoors, having supper. She thought of the little boy, Leroy, whose family lived in the apartment next to hers. He would often come and say hello and tug her into his kitchen so that she could share her evening meal with his family.

'Aren't you going to invite me in?' Carlos asked when she hesitated at the main door. 'I'd like to see where you live.'

'I would,' she said diffidently, 'but, to be honest, it's very cramped in my apartment, and the windows will have been closed up all day. The air-conditioning has broken down, and I'm not sure you'd be very comfortable.'

'Why don't you let me be the judge of that?' he said smoothly. He pushed open the large wooden door and ushered her into the hallway, a hand cupping her elbow.

'We'll have to take the stairs,' she told him. 'The lift isn't working either.' He had made up his mind to come with her, and there wasn't much she could do about that. It would have been plain bad manners to turn him away.

'Hi, Anna.' Eight-year-old Leroy popped his head round a corner of the stairwell and beamed at her, the whites of his eyes shining brightly in his chocolate brown face. 'You coming in for supper with us tonight?'

'Not tonight, Leroy,' she said with a smile. 'Thanks all the same, but I've a friend with me. I'll be round tomorrow perhaps, if your mother is happy about that.'

He nodded, grinning. 'She says you can come round any time…she's always got a stew pot on the stove. Plenty for everyone.' He looked at Carlos. 'Are you looking after Anna?' he asked pointedly. 'She needs someone. She's all on her own, except for that man who comes here sometimes. My mom reckons—'

'I'll talk to your mother later,' Anna cut in swiftly,

unlocking her door. 'Just tell her thanks for the screw-driver she lent me. I fixed the lock and it's fine now.'

'OK. See you later.' Still smiling, Leroy disap-peared into his own apartment.

'Sounds as though he has your welfare at heart,' Carlos murmured.

'They're nice people,' she said, pushing open the door. 'They've been really good to me since I arrived here.'

He followed her into the living room, and stood for a moment looking around at the plain walls, which she had enlivened with pretty water-colour paintings she had bought from one of the shops by the harbour.

Anna went over to the windows and pushed them open to let in the warm evening air. The scent of flowers drifted up from the window-boxes that some of the tenants had planted to add a touch of colour, and she breathed it in, trying to calm herself.

'Something's on your mind.' Carlos had followed her to the window, and now he stood close behind her, his dark head just a fraction away from hers. 'Tell me about it.'

'There's nothing to tell.'

'Isn't there?' He was sceptical. 'Why didn't you want me to come here?'

'I was afraid you wouldn't like it,' she said hon-estly. Her green glance was troubled. 'You and I are from such different backgrounds, and I've seen the way you live. We're worlds apart.'

He frowned. 'Does that matter?'

'I don't know. I suppose I'm uncomfortable about it.'

'Why should you be?'

With a soft sigh, she turned to face him properly. 'Perhaps you're not conscious of how much you have, compared with others. You have a beautiful house and your lifestyle probably echoes that. There's nothing wrong in that. You're very fortunate, and hardworking, too, but I worry about people who don't have the advantages you have, the people who can't afford to use your clinic...the Leroys of this world who simply get by the best way they can. His father catches fish for a living. They have very little, but they don't think twice about sharing what they have with me.'

'They may not have access to the clinic, but they can still get treatment at the hospital. They aren't losing out in any way. I do what I can for the hospital by working there and trying to raise funds for it through the Friends of the Hospital. I don't see how you can blame me for being privileged.'

'I don't blame you. You asked me why I felt uncomfortable bringing you here, and I'm trying to explain, that's all.'

His gaze narrowed on her. 'This doesn't have anything to do with wealth at all, does it? It's more to do with how you feel about me as an individual, as a man—isn't that the truth of it? Are you afraid you might be getting too close to me, is that it? Is that why you're putting up barriers?'

Her voice broke in a ragged laugh. 'You're wrong about that. Believe me, I have no interest in you at all. You're the last man I'd even look at. I have more in common with Tom than I do with you.'

For a moment his head went back and he looked as though she had slapped him, his expression one of stunned disbelief. Then, as he slowly recovered, his jaw moved in a way that could only spell trouble.

He said softly, 'Is that so?'

His gaze moved over her, a slow, totally masculine appraisal that took in every detail of her appearance, from the gleaming golden cascade of her hair right down to the smooth shapeliness of her long legs.

'Perhaps I should persuade you otherwise,' he growled. Then he was reaching for her, his hand possessively circling her slender waist and drawing her to him. His tawny glance travelled slowly upwards to the soft fullness of her mouth and lingered there.

She really should have seen it coming and tried to stop it, but in those few breathless moments her own gaze was transfixed, mesmerised by the heated promise in his glittering eyes as he pulled her closer still, crushing her feminine curves against the hard contours of his body.

And then it was too late, because his head bent closer and his mouth claimed hers in a kiss that was earth-shatteringly fierce. His lips moved possessively on hers, demanding, plundering the softness of her mouth as though he would take everything she had to offer. Unguarded, Anna's senses went haywire, her heartbeat thundering so loudly that she felt sure he must hear it. His arms closed around her, and the warm intimacy of his embrace was like a drug, swirling through her veins and going straight to her head.

She hadn't expected to feel such hectic confusion, or to find that her treacherous body would betray her in such a way, making her legs weak and insubstantial and her body melt against his in delicious, fluid response.

Then he dragged his mouth from hers and for a devastating second or two she felt the loss almost like a pain.

'Is this what you were afraid of?' he said raggedly, his breath warmly fanning her cheek. Then his mouth brushed hers once more, seductively enticing a quivering response, his tongue lightly tracing the soft contours of her lips, leaving a trail of fire and playing havoc with her emotions.

She had never known a kiss could be like this, stirring up everything that was primitive in her soul, making her eager for more. His body was hard and urgent against hers, searing in the intensity of its demand.

She felt him groan huskily, and as his kiss softened, gentled, she was lost to everything except the sweet invitation to respond. Her common sense, all her instincts, told her that this was wrong, but she paid them no attention. Instead, her body was pliant, supple, meshing with the hardness of his so that she could feel his strong thighs pressuring her, feel the urgent demand of his hands as they stroked and caressed her.

He made her feel wild and reckless, his kisses compelling her to respond with a fiery passion that she had never experienced before.

'You see how wrong you can be, *querida*?' His voice was thickened, rough around the edges. 'You say you feel nothing for me, yet your body clings to mine as though we were made for each other.'

She looked up at him in dismay, her green eyes wide and troubled. What was he saying? How could she have let him batter down her defences and leave her helpless like this? Oh, she was a fool, a crazy idiot, to let him get away with it.

She recognised the glimmer of mockery in his eyes, and it was like a knife, lancing her body. He had used her ruthlessly, and now he was taunting her, making her know just how reckless she had been.

'This was a mistake,' she said huskily. 'It should never have happened.' Sick with herself, she pushed him away. It was enough that she had to battle with her emotions, without having him stand there and watch her do it. 'I want you to go.'

He stared at her, a nerve flicking along the line of his jaw. 'Perhaps you're right,' he muttered thickly. 'Things got out of hand. They should never have gone this far.'

He turned away from her, and strode briskly to the door. She heard it close behind him and only then did she take a shuddery breath and acknowledge how hurt she felt.

Wretchedly, she realised just how big a mistake she had made. He would never want someone like her, would he? She had challenged his masculinity and he had set out to make her see the error of her ways, that was all.

She pulled in a shaky breath. She had learned a lesson, hadn't she? She wouldn't make the same mistake again.

CHAPTER SEVEN

ANNA didn't see much of Carlos over the next couple of weeks, and life was hectic at the hospital so that when she went home in the evening she was too tired to do much more than fall into bed. More often than not she would be asleep almost as soon as her head touched the pillow.

On Friday, two little girls were brought in with symptoms of vomiting and diarrhoea, and both of them were looking really poorly. Anna quickly ordered tests so that she could find out what causing their illness.

'These infants look in a bad way.' Carlos appeared as she was checking on the children. He frowned, looking down at the huddled little figures in the cots and scanning their sweat dampened features. 'Was it something they've eaten?'

'Probably,' she answered, wondering what had brought him on to the ward. 'I'll know more about what's happening when I get the results of the blood tests. In the meantime, I'm rehydrating them by giving them glucose electrolyte solution and intravenous fluids.'

'Analgesics, too?'

'Yes. They've been given something for the pain. They've been complaining that their joints and muscles are hurting, according to the mother. Both of them are very weak.'

'Blood tests could take some time. Sometimes the earlier treatment is started, the better chance we have of dealing with it.'

'I know.' She grimaced. Toxin induced diarrhoea could be a major cause of infantile death in some parts of the world, and she desperately wanted to find a quick solution. 'It isn't something I've come across before, so I want to be sure of my facts before I start any other treatment.'

'Are there any other symptoms?'

'Numbness and tingling around the mouth—I think their hands and feet have been affected, too.'

'Hmm…was their last meal fish?'

She nodded. 'Yes. I can't be certain what fish in particular, because there were several different types in the same dish.'

'It's a pity they are too young to answer questions with any degree of accuracy. There is one toxin that causes a reversal of sensation…something hot feels cold, and vice versa. It would simplify the diagnosis if we knew what their sensations were.'

Anna felt a ray of hope. 'Trina told her mother that she had burnt herself on the cold water tap. At the time I thought she was confused because she was such a small child, still learning how to talk, and she might not really understand the difference between the words "hot" and "cold". Children do muddle them sometimes, don't they?'

He smiled. 'They do, but in this case it could be that she had it right. I think we may be dealing with ciguatera. There's a medication that's effective if given in the early stages. Shall we give it a try?'

'Yes, of course. The sooner the better.'

Following his advice, she wrote out the medication chart and handed it to Maria. 'Start the dosage straight away, Maria, and we'll do observations every fifteen minutes. Let me know if there's any change.'

'Leave it to me.' Maria hurried to get the antidote, her shining bob of dark hair swinging lightly as she turned away, and Anna walked back to the office with Carlos.

She was feeling uneasy about having to rely on him to come up with the diagnosis, and maybe he realised that because he said softly, 'Don't blame yourself for not getting to know the cause of the illness straight away. The blood tests will confirm it, but I've dealt with this form of poisoning far more often than you.'

'I didn't think it was that prevalent these days,' she murmured.

'That's true, in a way, but sometimes micro-organisms are thrown up from the ocean floor after a storm, and go on to cause toxins in fish like snapper, or grouper and barracuda. Most fishermen know to avoid areas where the toxin is to be found, but they're not infallible.'

'I suppose I'll know better next time.'

'That's true.' He sent her an oblique glance. 'I wanted to thank you again for helping out with Joseph at the clinic.'

'How is he? I wanted to go over to the clinic to see him, but most evenings I've been working late and there just hasn't been the opportunity.'

'He's not very strong, but he's been asking about you. He wants to know why you don't work at the clinic.'

She smiled at that. 'I suppose he's used to seeing you appear at both the hospital and the clinic, and he thinks we might all do the same. Tell him I'm thinking about him, will you? I'll go and see him when things are less frantic here.'

'I'll do that. Have you remembered the barbecue tomorrow?'

She nodded. 'Yes, I have thought about it. I'll be working for some of the time, but I'll try to come along and show my face.'

On Saturday afternoon, Anna went to see Nick again. It was the first opportunity she'd had to visit since that last evening when Daniel had been asleep because Nick had been too busy to arrange a time that suited him.

Now, though, he let her into the house, and showed her through to the living room, saying cautiously, 'I wasn't sure whether you would come today. It's the Friends of the Hospital barbecue this afternoon, isn't it?'

'Oh, it'll be going on until late this evening,' she murmured. 'I won't be missed for a while. Besides, I had to work this morning, and I wanted to come here before I did anything else.' She glanced at his taut features. 'How are you?'

'Still busy,' he said laconically. 'I'm having the hotel restaurant extended, and I'm having to supervise a lot of the work.'

'I heard about that,' she said. 'From what people say, it's going to look really good when the work's finished.'

'That's the general idea.'

Even though they had arranged this meeting, she sensed that he was in no mood for small talk and she said thoughtfully, 'Where's Daniel? Is he playing outside?'

'No.' He paused, and regarded her steadily. 'He isn't here.'

She stared at him, not quite taking in what he was saying and feeling as though she had been winded. 'But when I phoned, you said that I would be able to see him. I was really looking forward to it—it's been such a long time since I was able to talk to him. What happened?' A sudden thought struck her. 'He isn't ill, is he? I know he was feverish last time I was here, but I thought he had got over that…you didn't say anything had happened.'

'He's gone to a friend's house. I didn't think it was a good idea for you to see him. It will only upset him and make him unsettled. He's getting used to being here with me, and I don't want him disturbed right now.'

Anna felt as though he had punched her. She felt the blood drain from her face, and after she had taken a moment or two to recover from the shock, she said huskily, 'How could you do that? Do you understand how cruel you're being? Not just to Daniel and Sarah, but to the rest of his family. Don't you realise that I care about him as well, and so do his grandparents? Don't we matter to you at all?'

His eyes darkened. 'You think I'm being selfish, don't you? Well, maybe I am. But while you're all so concerned about your own feelings, who is going to listen to my rights, my needs as a father?'

'No one has said that you don't have any rights, or that we don't want to listen. We all want to work things out for the best. Can't you see that—can't you at least try to meet us halfway?'

His mouth firmed. 'I want my son with me, Anna. Like it or not, I've made up my mind and that's how it's going to be. There's nothing more to be said.'

He wasn't giving any ground, no matter what she said to try to persuade him to see reason, and she left the house just a short time later, feeling more upset than she had been in a long time. Worse still, what on earth was she going to say to Sarah? How could she tell her that he wasn't even prepared to listen?

She didn't feel at all like going along to the barbecue now. The last thing she wanted was to have to mix with people and make light-hearted conversation, but how could she get out of it? The whole thing had been arranged in order to gather in funds for the hospital, and it would look bad if she wasn't there. Perhaps she could put in an appearance for just a short time, and then slip quietly away.

The barbecue was in full swing when she finally arrived there at the end of the afternoon. The area that had been marked out for the event was set back a little from the beach on a partially terraced area, shaded to one side from the fierce heat of the day by a latticed wooden sun screen, around which foliage sprawled, adding a touch of tropical greenery.

The smell of cooked steaks and spiced chicken floated on the air. The thought of food made her feel ill, and she wondered if she could stay on the sidelines for a while, looking on, and not have to talk to anyone for a while. Her optimism was short-lived.

'Hello,' Tom said, coming across to her. 'You look hot and bothered. Shall I fetch you a glass of fruit juice?'

'Thanks. That would be good.'

He brought it to her and they went and stood under the cover of an awning, where a fan had been set up to cool the air.

Anna looked around. To one side, against a background of tilting palms and banana trees, she could see stalls offering goods for sale—items of clothing, jewellery or bric-à-brac—and people were browsing, or stopping to buy something that caught their fancy.

There was entertainment, too. A trio of musicians had set up on a section of raised decking, pouring out songs with a lively salsa rhythm. Under normal circumstances she might have enjoyed listening to the sounds and perhaps joining in, but right now she felt numb inside after her meeting with Nick.

Her glance moved to the side of the bandstand, and she suddenly felt as though her heart had slammed against her chest wall when she saw that Carlos was standing there.

He wasn't alone, though. He had his arm around the waist of a young woman, and his head was bent close to hers as she smiled up at him. She was wearing a beautifully cut linen suit, tailored to emphasise a perfect figure. Her dark, shining hair was woven into an attractive pleat at the back, and as she lifted a hand to run her fingers lightly down his shirt front, Anna saw that her nails were smoothly manicured and painted with a gloss that matched the vivid coral lipstick she wore.

Anna watched their absorption in each other with a rapidly sinking heart and felt drab in comparison. Her mouth suddenly felt unusually dry, and she took a careful sip of her drink, letting the cool liquid moisten her parched throat.

'That's our consultant's girlfriend,' Tom said, following her glance. 'Francesca. She's quite something, isn't she?'

'She's beautiful,' Anna agreed, a horrible sick feeling starting in the pit of her stomach. 'What makes you think they're back together again?'

'He's been seeing a lot of her lately. You know what the hospital grapevine's like. No one can keep anything quiet for long.'

That was true enough, and she was already wishing that she hadn't asked. She didn't want to think about Carlos's love life.

Her glance strayed back to him and the woman, and she saw that there was a small boy with them. He suddenly appeared from behind Francesca and tugged on her jacket, claiming her attention. He was around two years old, small and thin-looking, with black hair and golden skin tones. He looked tired, and she watched as Carlos lifted the boy up into his arms.

'I didn't realise that she had a child,' she said, puzzled. 'I thought you said she was going to marry Carlos?'

'She was, as far as I know. I don't know all the details but, from what I've heard, he and Francesca have been linked for as far back as they can remember. They come from two of the oldest established families around here. I know he thinks the world of her.'

It wasn't surprising that Carlos was drawn to her. Apart from being attractive and beautifully groomed, she would fit in very well with his social scene. They were two of a kind, from the looks of things, and for some strange reason the knowledge stuck in Anna's throat.

'So what happened? Did she marry someone else?'

'I'm not sure about that. I know she met someone and went away for a time, and Carlos seemed to be completely thrown by that. Just a few months ago, though, she came back, and to everyone's surprise she had a child with her. There was no sign of the man, so the word is that it all fell through. I suppose that's why Carlos has taken up with her again.'

Tom was probably right. If he had loved her from the beginning, why would that have changed if she had been the one to break it off? Anna struggled to push all thoughts of the two…three…of them to the back of her mind. It knotted her stomach to think of them together.

Tom shifted restlessly. 'Let's go and sit down at one of the tables, shall we? I haven't eaten since lunchtime, and I'm getting hungry now, aren't you?'

She wasn't. Between her session with Nick and now seeing Carlos in intimate conversation with another woman she was beginning to feel pretty wretched. She wished the evening would end.

Tom filled plates with a selection of food for both of them, adding fresh mango and pineapple to her tray for dessert, and took them over to a table where they could sit on the terrace and watch the sea roll in over the smooth sand.

They sat there for some time, and Anna tried her very best to relax. She sipped her chilled fruit juice and looked out over the tranquil water and wished that life could be simple and easier to handle.

Then Carlos's deep voice broke in on her thoughts, smoothing over her senses like dark chocolate, and she blinked, looking up at him. He was with Saskia, and Anna wondered where his woman friend had gone. 'You looked as though you were miles away,' he murmured.

'Did I?' Why did he have to be so incredibly male and set all her senses humming? He was dressed casually, in an open necked blue shirt and perfectly cut cream trousers that emphasised his powerful, long legs.

She quickly dragged her gaze away from him and looked at his sister instead. 'Hello, Saskia. Why don't you come and sit down? You look hot.'

Carlos pulled out a chair for her, and Saskia sat down, easing her bump into a comfortable position. 'I'm whacked,' she said. 'I don't know why I ever got myself in this state in this climate.'

Carlos's brow quirked. 'Don't you?' he murmured, and she grinned, slapping him light-heartedly with the back of her hand.

He sat down beside Anna, and said, 'I wondered if you would get here at all today. I know you were working this morning, but I wasn't sure what time you were finishing. I was called away, otherwise I'd have given you a lift.'

'There was no need and, anyway, I had to go to see Nick before I came here. Besides, I have my own car now. I followed your advice and rang the garage. They were very good, and they found me a decent little runabout that suits me really well. It gives me a bit more independence and saves me a lot of time, not having to get the bus when Tom's shifts don't coincide with mine.'

His eyes darkened. 'I'm glad that's all sorted.'

Tom said lightly, 'We saw you with your friend by the bandstand earlier. Do you want to bring her over to sit with us? We can soon find some more chairs.'

Carlos shook his head. 'I took Fran home a few minutes ago. Ben was getting fractious with the heat, and she wanted to get him to bed. She's been here for most of the afternoon, so she doesn't feel she'll be missing out.'

Saskia murmured, 'Carlos had to come back here to call the raffle. It was a bit of a rush.'

She and Tom started to chat quietly, and Anna let her attention wander. The little boy had looked tired, as though he'd been ready for bed, and it had prob-ably been natural for Carlos to offer to take them home. Would he have stayed with Francesca if he hadn't been obliged to come back here? But she wasn't going to dwell on that...it provoked too many dismaying possibilities.

Her thoughts swerved to Sarah. How was she going to tell her sister about this afternoon's visit to Nick? Sarah would relish the opportunity to be able to take her child home and put him to bed. It was far too upsetting to have to let her know that the day when she might have her son back was even more distant than they had imagined.

Perhaps she wouldn't mention the visit to her. She would wait until she had better news.

'So what's on your mind?' She jerked her gaze upwards to find Carlos studying her with narrowed eyes. 'From the first moment I saw you this afternoon, I had the feeling that something's wrong. You look as though you wish you were anywhere but here.'

'Do I?' She winced. 'I'm fine. Just a little tired, probably. I've just worked a seven-day stretch, and I'm ready for a couple of days off.'

'Are you having problems at work?'

'No, not really. It's been hectic, but so far it seems to be going well. I discharged little Jessie, and last week I let Jack go home. He was coping better with the hepatitis but, of course, he'll need to take things slowly for some weeks to come.'

He nodded. 'Grace was over the moon when she had Jessie back home.' He studied her keenly. 'You were fond of Jessie, weren't you? I could see it in your eyes when you looked at her in her cot. I was worried that you might be getting too involved again.'

Anna tried a shrug. 'It's hard not to get attached to them. It tears me apart when I see them looking so helpless and ill, but when they start to recover they can be bright and lively and chirpy as ever within a very short time. That's the best part about this job.'

Saskia sighed heavily, and Anna glanced in her direction. She was gazing wistfully at the people who were dancing on a small circle of wooden flooring in front of the bandstand. 'How do they find the energy?' she muttered woefully. 'I can't wait to get myself back in trim again and join the real world. All I want to do just lately is sit and vegetate.'

Carlos leaned over and squeezed her shoulder gently. 'You've only a couple of weeks to go,' he said cheerfully. 'You'll be back on form in no time at all.'

'Promises, promises.' She looked from one to the other of them. 'Why don't you two go and dance? I need to sit here and rest my bones, but you don't have to.'

Carlos quirked a brow at Anna. 'Would you like to dance?'

'Oh…' She was taken aback by the suggestion. 'I thought I might just sit here and keep Tom and Saskia company.'

Saskia shook her head. 'We're perfectly happy as we are and, anyway, Tom's going to fetch some more drinks. It's not often I get the chance to relax without Sebastian, and it's a huge relief just to sit here and do nothing. He's gone to a party of his own today.' She flapped a hand at them. 'Go on, both of you.' She reached into her bag and drew out a fan to waft a cooling breeze over her hot face.

Carlos held out his hand, and Anna found herself being drawn to her feet and fluidly manoeuvred in place beside him. His other hand went around her waist, and she felt as though her skin were on fire, his touch provoking warm and tingling sensations that rampaged through every part of her.

The music changed, softened to a slow, lazily sensual rhythm, and he held her close so that they moved as one on the tiny dance floor. The gentle pressure of his hard thighs nudging hers made her feel dizzy and out of control, and her limbs felt light and insubstantial. It was just as well that he wasn't letting go of her. He swung her gently round in time with the music, their bodies merged in delicious intimacy.

'I know something's on your mind,' he said softly. 'Tell me what it is. I want to know. I want to help.'

'I already told you, there's nothing.'

He shook his head. 'I know you, Anna. I can sense when something's troubling you. If it isn't work, what is it? Is it Nick? You said you went to see him this afternoon—how did it go?'

'He was busy…he didn't really have any time to spare,' she said quietly. 'It wasn't a good time to see him.'

Carlos frowned. 'Wasn't he expecting you?'

'Yes, but…' She took a deep breath and said shakily, 'I think he had changed his mind. He didn't really want me there.'

'Because of your nephew?'

She said huskily, 'I think so. He's afraid that Daniel will be confused and upset if he sees me. I wouldn't want that…but I think Nick's wrong. I think Daniel would be happy to know that I care about him, that his mother cares about him. I just… Somehow I just don't seem to be able to get through to Nick…' She broke off, biting her lip. 'I don't expect you to understand. You're his friend, you know how he feels. You sympathise with him, don't you?'

'That doesn't mean I can't see your point of view. You're his sister-in-law, part of his family now, and he owes you a hearing at least. I'll talk to him for you.'

'No, don't do that. I…I can handle this myself. I don't need you to intervene on my behalf. I can manage.'

The music came to an end, and when she would have moved away from him he reached for her, his hands gripping her arms. 'Why won't you let me do this for you, Anna? I can help, I know I can.'

She shook her head. How could she let him risk losing a friendship that went back over several years? 'This is my problem,' she said thickly. 'I'll sort it out.'

She twisted away from him. 'Look, I've had a difficult day, and I think I'll go home now. I need to get away, to think things through on my own.'

'Anna, wait…' He would have come after her, but someone stopped him, wanting a word, and she took her chance and hurried away.

She said a swift goodbye to Tom and Saskia, who looked surprised but accepted her excuse that it had been a long day and she needed to go home and take a cool shower.

Within minutes she was in her car and heading back along the road towards Blue Water Bay.

Back at her apartment, Leroy's mother, Bea, met her at the door, looking agitated, and Anna wondered what on earth could have happened.

'Oh, my, oh, my…it's chaos everywhere,' Bea

said, throwing up her hands. 'Old Roback left his tap running upstairs, and went away for a few days!' She shook her head. 'I think there's a big, big problem. You come and see.'

Not knowing what to expect, Anna cautiously opened her door and they trooped inside. The damage was plain to see as soon as she went into her living room. Water had seeped through the ceiling and it must have been going on for a great length of time because the plasterboard had given way and most of what had once been a ceiling had crashed down onto Anna's floor.

She stared at the mess in stunned silence. That was all she needed to end the day.

'I thought he'd made a big problem,' Bea put in. 'What are you going to do, Anna?'

Bemused, Anna said in a thickened voice, 'I'm not sure right now, Bea. I think I need time to take it in.'

'I bet you've got no electricity either,' Bea muttered, looking up at the shattered central light fitting. 'I'll cook for you tonight and tomorrow.' She shook her head at the sight of it all. 'Leroy's going to be mad that he's not here… He's gone away to visit with his friends. He went on the boat yesterday.'

She paused, then added on a worried note, 'I heard rumours there was dengue starting up in the north. I sure hope he keeps away from the mosquitoes.'

Anna frowned. The virus was spread by a species of mosquito that usually bred in small containers that collected rainwater, like discarded plastic boxes or earthenware jars or even used tyres. Most towns had a policy of encouraging people to be careful about leaving such things lying about, so that the habitats for the mosquitoes would die out. Insecticides were used, too, to try to eradicate them.

With any luck, Leroy wasn't anywhere near the area where the outbreak had occurred and, anyway, he would be back home in a day or so.

All the same, she said quietly, 'I expect he'll be fine. Just keep an eye on him when he gets back, and if there's any sign of vomiting and diarrhoea, or fever, get him straight to a doctor.'

They heard footsteps on the stairs, and then there was a sharp knock on the apartment door. Anna went to open it and found Carlos standing there, his hand resting impatiently on the doorframe. Dazedly, she looked at him, not able to take in the fact that he was actually here at the apartment.

'You left in such a hurry,' he said, 'but I couldn't let you go off like that without finding out if there was something I could do. We need to talk.'

Slowly, her mind began to clear, and she pulled the door open wider. 'You'd better come in.'

Bea came into the hallway and nodded to Carlos, before saying, 'I got to go and see to something on the stove. You let me know what you're going to do.'

'I will. Thanks, Bea.'

Carlos stepped aside to let Bea go out, then looked searchingly at Anna. 'You're still in a state, aren't you? I can see it in your eyes.'

'I've just had a bit of a shock,' she murmured, 'that's why.' He frowned, and she added resignedly, 'Come and see for yourself.'

She took him through to the living room and he stood and looked around, his eyes widening.

'Well, this is certainly a mess, isn't it?' he said

finally. 'You can't stay here, not with things in this state.'

'I don't know what to do yet. Bea's just offered to cook for me, but if it's going to be like this for some time… Presumably the landlord has insurance to cover this kind of event, but putting it right could take a while.' She frowned, thinking things through. 'I suppose I could always take Tom up on his offer.'

Carlos's gaze narrowed on her. 'What offer was that?'

She said slowly, 'When the air-conditioning broke down here, he said I could stay at his place.'

'That wouldn't be a very wise thing to do. I know you and he seem to be getting on very well, but it could be a bad time for you to decide to move in with him. He's supposed to be studying for specialist exams that are coming up soon. He needs to concentrate his mind, not give himself up to distractions.'

She had forgotten about Tom's forthcoming exams. Even so, she wasn't sure how to take Carlos's warning. His words had an edge to them and she wasn't too happy at being told she would be in the way.

'You're assuming that me being there would be a problem, but I don't see myself as being a difficult house guest, and Tom obviously doesn't. He must have thought about it before he made the suggestion.'

His mouth twisted derisively. 'I think it's highly unlikely that Tom has thought it through at all beyond the fact that he'd be more than glad to have you around. He's hardly to blame for that. He's young, and still inclined to be hot headed, and you're a stunningly attractive young woman. It's no wonder he can't think straight these days.'

She was taken aback by his words. Stunningly attractive? She blinked and said, 'I hadn't noticed him having any problems.'

'You wouldn't have. You walk on through the hospital, getting on with your job, without seeing the trail of broken hearts you leave behind.'

Her eyes widened. 'I haven't a clue what you're talking about. You're making this up, aren't you?'

His tawny eyes flashed. 'I'm not making anything up. I wish I was. I see it every day when I go on my ward rounds.' A hint of impatience came into his voice. 'If it isn't the adult patients who are bemoaning the fact that you aren't their doctor, it's the junior doctors who can't keep their minds on what they're supposed to be doing. It's almost reached a point where I feel like banning you from walking through my wards. I'd hate my patients to have heart attacks before I've had the chance to operate on them.'

Her mouth had dropped open in astonishment, and he reached out and tilted her jaw with his forefinger, before brushing his thumb gently over the fullness of her lower lip. His touch was feather-light, but it created ripples of sensation that flowed right through her down to her toes and made them curl.

'This, too,' he murmured, 'is just an example of what I mean. You have a very pretty mouth, Anna, and it is far too much of a temptation around here.'

Abruptly she clamped it shut again in sheer surprise, and he laughed softly. 'So, I'm getting through to you at last, am I? That's good.'

Carlos ran a gleaming glance over her. 'Now, what's to be done about your accommodation? We

can't have you falling over plaster debris and work-
men when you have an important job of work to do.'

'I could look into finding myself a room at the
hospital, I suppose.' She would have to remind Tom
about his exams, and explain that she didn't want to
get in the way of his studying. 'There's probably a
place where I can at least sleep, and then I could get
my meals at the hospital.'

He shook his head. 'That won't do at all, Anna.
Those rooms are poky and miserable, and you don't
need to put up with having to live in one of them.
You can stay at my house. There's plenty of room
there, and Martha will be glad to have someone else
to appreciate her cooking.'

He gently turned her towards the living-room door.
'Go and pack a few things and I'll take you home
with me.'

She looked at him in a bewildered fashion. 'You
want me to go home with you?'

'That's what I said.' His eyes glinted. 'It's a big
house and there's plenty of room in it for both of us.
I hope you weren't planning on giving me an argument about that?'

She wasn't even able to think straight right now,
let alone give him an argument. Somehow, though,
she did have the feeling that she was being steam-
rollered all over again.

CHAPTER EIGHT

CARLOS was clearly waiting for an answer, and Anna said hurriedly, 'I wouldn't want to put you out at all. I know how busy you are and, besides, it might not look too good, with you being the consultant here. People might talk…'

She was conscious that she was babbling, but the thought of staying with him for any length of time, of being so close to him for any time at all, was making her uncommonly nervous.

His brow rose. 'People can say whatever they want…but preferably they'll say it to me and then I shall put them right. That shouldn't worry you.'

'That's easy for you to say.'

'If it bothers you, you can be comfortable with the fact that Martha will be around to act as a chaperone. People will have no cause to comment. It's all completely open and above board, as they say.'

Anna thought about that. In part it was true. Martha would be there most of the time, though she had her own home to go to when she had finished work.

Still uncertain, she said quietly, 'Perhaps you're right. I don't know how long it will be before the apartment will be straight again, and the hospital rooms aren't meant for more than an overnight stay. I'll have to think it through.'

'There's nothing more to think about.'

'Isn't there?'

'Nothing at all.'

He made it sound as though only a mad person would refuse. 'Well...I suppose, if it won't be any trouble to you, then...yes, I will. Thank you.'

'*De nada.* You're welcome.'

He had it all worked out, didn't he? She only hoped she was doing the right thing in letting him talk her into it.

He waited while she hurriedly packed the things that she thought she might need.

'It's going to take some clearing up in here,' he said, casting a glance over the gaping hole in the ceiling and the damage that the water had done to the furniture and flooring.

'It looks as if this has been ruined,' she muttered, holding up the radio that had been on a table and had now been rendered useless. 'Funnily enough, I think I'll miss that as much as anything. I like to listen to the music while I'm getting ready for work in the morning. I wander round in my robe and get breakfast and so on, and the music helps me to relax and makes me feel good.'

'I can imagine,' he murmured, and she thought she caught a glimmer of something in his eyes, but it was gone a second later. Perhaps she had been mistaken.

'Are you ready now?' he said a few minutes later, when she took a final glance around.

Anna nodded. 'I think so. I can't think of anything I might have forgotten.'

'You should find whatever you need at my house,' he said evenly. 'If not, just let me know.'

'You've been good enough to me already. Thank you. I'll just go and say goodbye to Bea.'

While she did that, Carlos carried the cases out to his car and locked them in the boot, then came to help her into the passenger seat.

'I thought I would follow in my car,' she said, but he lifted a dark brow at that.

'I can give you a lift to and from work every day. It seems a waste to use both cars when we will be heading in the same direction.'

Perhaps there was some sense in what he was saying... Anyway, it would only be for a few days, with a bit of luck.

They took the road to the harbour, and Carlos said lightly, 'Martha will be pleased to see you. She's been full of admiration for you since you looked after little Jessie.'

He gave his attention to the road then, and it wasn't long before they arrived at his house. He parked the car on the wide drive, and ushered her inside.

True enough, Martha was in her element when Anna walked into the kitchen a minute or so later.

'Well, look at you,' the older woman exclaimed. 'Aren't you as skinny as ever? We've got to feed you up now you're here.'

She came over and gave Anna a huge hug that very nearly squeezed the breath out of her. Out of the corner of her eye, Anna caught Carlos's gleam of amusement, and her own mouth twitched.

'That's for lookin' after my Jessie. She was so poorly we didn't know what to do. But she beautiful now, thanks to you. She's my little angel, you know. I don't know what I would do without her.'

'I'm really glad she's well again, Martha,' Anna said with a smile, when she could breathe again after Martha had released her from the hug. 'But, you know, it was Carlos who brought her to me. He knew that she needed to be in hospital, and he was the one who made sure she was looked after properly.'

'Maybe…but he knows you are a good doctor. He knew you would take care of her.'

There was no telling Martha that she had only done what any competent doctor would have done. She was determined to give Anna the de luxe treatment.

There was so much food on offer for supper that she had to refuse seconds, saying laughingly, 'I couldn't manage another thing, Martha, honestly.'

'We'll take our coffee out onto the balcony,' Carlos suggested when they had cleared away. 'Come and sit awhile and get some air.'

They went through to the lounge, and this time the glass doors were wide open, leading onto polished wooden decking. There was a hammock seat out there, and Anna settled herself on it, looking out in wonder over the magnificent view of the harbour below them. Huddled around the harbour were rolling hills, covered in lush tropical growth, eventually giving way to the steeper slopes of mountains in the background.

'It's beautiful,' she murmured, breathing in the fragrant air and feeling the warmth of the evening sun on her bare arms. 'It must make you feel so liberated to be able to come and sit out here whenever you want, and just take in the view.'

'It does,' he answered, and there was an odd huskiness about his voice that drew her attention. She glanced up and caught his steady, enigmatic gaze, and wondered what he was thinking. He certainly wasn't taking in the landscape. But then he came to sit beside her and her mind fizzed into overdrive, thrown by his nearness.

As he settled himself, he stretched taut muscles, and she was instantly and heart-stoppingly aware of his long legs and of the warmth that emanated from his body, just a fraction away from hers.

To distract herself, she gazed out over the mountains. If she looked carefully, she could just make out a sand coloured building in the distance. 'Is that the clinic?' she asked.

'It is,' he murmured, stretching an arm out casually along the back of the hammock.

Awareness prickled along the back of Anna's neck. She felt his closeness as though he had actually touched her, and her heart began to thud in erratic response. He was totally relaxed, though, and she wondered if he had any idea at all what this intimacy was doing to her.

'How is Joseph?' she asked, dragging her mind away from such dangerous ground. 'You said yesterday that he wasn't very strong. Isn't he recovering as he should?'

'He has a chest infection,' Carlos answered carefully. 'He's been worrying us a bit over these last couple of days.'

'Oh, no...' Her pulse quickened. 'That's the last thing he needs right now.'

'I've been concerned from the outset that he would succumb to something like this. We gave him antibiotics, but his lungs still filled with fluid. We're giving him a more powerful drug now, to deal with the infection more aggressively. I'm hoping that he's beginning to respond to the treatment at last. He doesn't have a lot of energy, of course, being so thin and small for his age, and he tires very easily. He needs building up carefully, so that he'll be able to fight these things.'

She frowned. He was such a lovely little boy, and she would dearly love to see him smile again. 'I must go and see him soon. Would that be all right?'

'Of course. I'm sure Joseph would like that, too.' He looked down at her, a faint smile hovering around his well-shaped mouth. 'You haven't changed at all, have you, in these last few weeks? You still care too much.' His glance trailed over her features, taking in the clear green of her eyes, and drifting down to rest lazily on her mouth.

'It is a very endearing quality, Anna. Even though it may lead you into heartache, your compassion shines through. No wonder your small patients love you.'

Somehow, without her knowing how it had happened, he seemed to have moved closer, much closer, to her, and then his head bent towards hers, blotting out the evening sunlight, and her gaze meshed with his.

His mouth brushed hers, gently, coaxingly, exploring the soft contours of her lips with a tender expertise that made her senses whirl. It was as though she had drunk too much of a fine wine and it had seeped into her bloodstream and was intent on causing havoc throughout her entire body.

He deepened the kiss, sliding an arm around her, his hand coming to rest lightly on the small span of her waist. She moved into the embrace, curling up against him in restless invitation, and his hand slid along the curve of her hip, shaping the line of her thighs and resting with sweet possessiveness in the hollow behind her knee.

She heard him mutter hoarsely, 'This has to be madness.' He lifted her closer, kissing her with a deepening passion that took her breath away.

It didn't seem like madness to her. It all seemed so right, so perfect, being with him like this, she thought hazily as his warm body pressed her into the soft cushions of the hammock. His kisses were urgent now, his lips tasting her mouth, her cheek, trailing over the sensitive column of her throat. His hand moved to cup the soft mound of her breast, and her body trembled, aching for more.

She felt him groan, a shuddery, thickened sound against the curve of her neck. She wanted this to go on for ever, but just as her body was melting into his, he shifted away from her.

'I'm sorry, Anna. This is all wrong. I didn't mean this to happen. I brought you here to help you, not for this.' He raked a hand through his hair and stared down at her, lines of strain beginning to show around his mouth.

Anna felt unutterably lost, defenceless against his sudden change of heart. When her mind began to clear at last, though, she thought she knew why he had drawn back.

'Are you still in love with Francesca?'

He stared at her in disbelief. 'Fran has nothing to do with this.'

'Doesn't she?' Anna looked into his eyes and saw the pain written there, and felt afraid, but still she persisted. 'You loved her once, didn't you?'

His mouth twisted. 'I suppose this is the grapevine at work, isn't it? Everybody talks, everyone thinks he knows everything there is to know.'

'Then tell me. Did you love her? Weren't you going to marry her? Can you tell me that isn't true?'

He grimaced. 'Fran and I have known each other since we were very small. I suppose I've always loved her in a way, and at one time there was talk of us perhaps getting married. It didn't work out that way and, anyway, she met someone else. End of story.'

'Is it? She's back in your life again, isn't she?' How could she ever hope to take the place of the woman who had been part of his life since childhood? The link was too strong to be broken.

'She came back here a few months ago, and she naturally comes to me for help and support. That doesn't mean that we've taken up where we left off, no matter what the grapevine says.'

But that might only be because Fran hadn't made up her mind what she wanted. The image of the two of them close together, his arm around her waist, came back to haunt her. 'You must have thought about how the two of you would go on when she came back.'

'Maybe I did,' he said in a roughened voice. 'Does it matter?'

'Yes, I think it does,' she said huskily. 'It means you haven't made up your mind yet about what it is that you want.'

'Look, Anna. I don't think this is something we can talk about now. It's late. You've had a difficult day, and I have work I must do before morning. We'll talk about this some other time, when perhaps we'll both make more sense of it. I'll see you at breakfast.'

She stared at him dazedly as he turned away from her. He hadn't denied thinking about starting over again with Francesca, had he? And he wasn't telling her that he had no feelings for her.

Breakfast? It would taste like ashes in her mouth. She had never felt so completely and utterly wretched in her life before. Was she making the biggest mistake of her life? Was she falling in love with him?

She made up her mind she wasn't going to question him about it again. Carlos would have to tell her whatever there was to know of his own accord.

Instead, the next morning at breakfast, she told him, 'I want to stop by the apartment and pick up my car.'

It wasn't a good time to mention it, because he was scowling and terse, and clearly running late for his appointments.

He said curtly, 'I hope you aren't thinking of going back to stay at the apartment.'

'No, it wasn't that.' Neither of them had mentioned

the previous evening, but it was there between them like a granite block. 'I want to go and visit Nick again some time, as well as Joseph, and I don't want to have to rely on you all the time for lifts.'

'As you please. You should be able to come and go whenever you like, of course.' He hesitated, as though he was about to say something else but then thought better of it. Instead, he added softly, 'By the way, don't wait supper for me tonight…I have to go out.'

He dropped her off on the way to work, and for the rest of the day she didn't see anything more of him. She went to bed before he returned home late that night, and she heard his car coming along the drive in the early hours of the morning. It was only then that she fell into an uneasy slumber.

'He's been to visit with that Francesca and her boy,' Martha told her in the morning, and Anna winced inwardly and wished she hadn't known that. It didn't help, to know that she had been right all along. Her mind worked overtime enough already, imagining them together.

'Is he sleeping in late today?' she asked, when Carlos didn't come down to the kitchen, but Martha shook her head.

'He had to make an early start. He's working at another of his hospitals today.'

'Oh, I see.' How on earth did he keep up the pace?

The evening followed a similar pattern. He took a phone call from José, and Anna realised from the tone of his conversation that he wasn't likely to be back until very late.

There was an uneasy pact between them in the days that followed, and Anna tried to keep herself busy whenever he was at home, finding things to do that would take her mind off him being around. It wasn't a problem that occurred too often. She was fast beginning to realise how hard he worked, dividing his time between the clinic and his various hospital consultancies…and Francesca, of course.

She went to see Nick again, taking a chance that he wouldn't turn her away. This time little Daniel, three years old and full of bubbly mischief, came running to the door to meet her as Nick opened it.

'Anna…' Daniel gazed at her, wide eyed, a big smile on his face, then said, 'Come and look. Come and see what I've got.' He grasped her hand and tugged her into the hallway, his hazel eyes shining.

'I will,' she said, giving him a smile in return. After all this time it was good to feast her eyes on her lively little nephew. 'Just give me a minute, livewire.' Above the child's head, Anna's gaze met Nick's. His eyes were dark, filled with restless impatience.

'I wondered how long it would be before you came back.' He grimaced. 'He'll show you everything we've gathered from every island we've visited,' he said. 'It will take for ever.'

He closed the front door behind her and she took the opportunity to study him afresh. Daniel took his features from his father—black hair, straight nose, the skin tone a pale bronze.

She gave an unsteady little laugh. 'It sounds as though he had a great time.'

'We both did. I like having my son with me. I'm

spending time with him, getting to know him all over again.' He looked at her steadily. 'I know why you're here, Anna, but I'm not ready to give him up without a fight.'

'I'm not suggesting that you give him up,' Anna said hurriedly. 'Only that you talk to Sarah and try to sort things out between you.'

His mouth twisted in an expression of scorn. 'Since when could Sarah and I talk without it finishing up in an argument?'

Anna sighed inwardly. This was going to be tougher than she could ever have imagined. He wasn't giving an inch, was he?

She tried a smile. 'I'm not asking a lot, am I? I thought that perhaps I could just see you and Daniel for a while. I'm living close by, I'm working at the hospital, and I just thought it would be good if I could see Daniel every now and again. Would that be all right?'

His features relaxed a fraction. 'If that's all you want—of course. Somehow, though, I doubt it.'

He ushered her along the wide hall towards a door at the end. 'Come on through to the study. You'll have to start off in there, anyway. Daniel wants to show you his collection.'

'We went to the coral reefs,' Daniel chimed in. 'And we went in a...' He looked at his father for clarification.

'A glass-bottomed boat,' Nick supplied. 'It was good fun, wasn't it?'

'Yes...and then we went to the beach and we found some shells...' Again he looked at Nick.

'Conch shells. Go and fetch them, then you can show Anna properly.'

Anna stayed with them for an hour, and she was relieved that at least she had been able to see Daniel and she would be able to phone Sarah and tell her that he was looking well.

She hadn't got anywhere at all with Nick. There was no softening in his attitude at all. He wouldn't even consider phoning Sarah and talking over the situation with her. As to letting Daniel talk to his mother, he was dismissive, saying curtly, 'That would only cause more problems. Daniel is happy as he is. Talking to Sarah would only make him upset.'

She couldn't reason with him, and she made a tactical withdrawal, satisfied for the moment that at least he had agreed to let her come back and visit on a regular basis.

'We've a patient coming in by ambulance,' Maria said on Wednesday morning. 'Suspected dengue fever, according to his doctor, with haemorrhagic complications. You know there was an outbreak in one of the northern islands?'

Alarm bells went off in Anna's head. 'Yes, I'd heard. Who is it?'

'His name's Leroy,' Maria said, her blue eyes frowning. 'Eight years old. Apparently he went to the island for a visit friends, and he returned home a couple of days ago.'

'Leroy?' Anna repeated in a whisper. She felt for the chair behind her and put a hand on it for support.

'That's right.' Maria looked up from the notes she

had been reading. 'You look shocked—why? Do you know him?'

'Does he live on Blue Water Bay?'

Maria nodded, and Anna felt a pain as though she had been kicked in the stomach. 'Yes. I know him,' she said hoarsely. She turned quickly, heading for the office, her stomach suddenly beginning to churn. 'I'll go and make the arrangements for his admission right away. He'll need to be nursed in isolation if the doctor is right about the complications. We'll need to use infection-control measures.'

Carlos walked into the office as she finished making the arrangements. He took one look at her face and said, 'What's wrong? What's happened?' She must have looked deathly pale, because he pulled out a seat and lightly pushed her down into it. 'Whatever it is, you'd better sit down and take a few moments.'

'I haven't time. The ambulance is on its way...' She looked up at him, anxiety clouding her green eyes. 'The little boy who lives in the apartment next to mine is coming in with suspected dengue haemorrhagic fever. I need to be ready to care for him. He's a lovely boy,' she added in a whisper. 'Always full of fun.'

She hesitated, then said, 'I've never dealt with this illness before, and the consultant in charge isn't answering his phone. I have to get this right, Carlos, but I'm too close to him, and all at once I'm feeling scared that I won't be able to do it.'

He put a hand on her shoulder and squeezed gently in a comforting gesture. 'You will. You're a good doctor, Anna. Have faith in yourself. You'll know what to do.' His brows met in a dark line. 'Is the boy in shock?'

'I don't know.' They both knew that the illness caused bleeding which could result in fatal shock if the child's systems shut down. The best chance for his survival was if they managed to recognise the signs of impending shock early and took measures to prevent it.

She took a deep breath. 'So far, all we have to go on is the report that the doctor phoned in. Leroy was complaining of an intense headache, and pains in his muscles and joints. He has a very high fever.'

'I'll come with you to the ambulance,' he said. 'We'll do this together.'

'Thanks, Carlos.' She was shaky, in shock herself, and she knew she had to prepare herself adequately for what was to come. 'I'm glad you're here with me,' she said unevenly, getting to her feet. With him by her side, she would be stronger.

He nodded, putting an arm around her shoulders, and together they went out to the main doors of the hospital to meet the ambulance.

The paramedics wheeled the boy out on a trolley and trundled him towards the building. Anna looked at Leroy quickly, assessing him visually.

Beads of sweat were breaking out on his face, and there was a discharge from his eyes, the result of conjunctivitis, another feature of the illness. He was mumbling something, though Anna couldn't tell what he was saying.

'Are you hurting?' she asked him, leaning closer, and he nodded.

She stroked his head lightly. 'I'll give you some-thing to take the pain away,' she told him sympa-thetically. 'Don't worry, Leroy. We'll look after you.'

His young face looked drawn, and she could un-derstand why. The local people sometimes called the illness breakbone fever.

'This is Mr Barrantes,' she told him. 'We're going to take you up to a room now, where we can make you more comfortable.'

Leroy's mother climbed down from the ambulance, and Anna gave her a quick hug.

'Is he going to be all right?' Bea asked anxiously. 'He's been vomiting and he had bad diarrhoea. I took him to the doctor straight away, like you said, but this happened very quickly.'

Anna's face was strained as she looked at Bea. 'I promise you, we'll do our very best for him, Bea. Let's get him up to his room as quickly as we can, and I'll examine him.'

As soon as they had transferred him to the bed in his room, she made a swift, gentle examination. 'His liver's enlarged,' she told Carlos quietly, 'and there's congestion on his lungs. His skin's bruised from the bleeding inside.'

'That's what we would have expected,' he ac-knowledged. 'Let's get him onto intravenous fluids right away to replace the fluid he's lost.'

She nodded, and turned to Maria, who was busy taking the boy's temperature and pulse. 'We'll give him oxygen as well to help with his breathing, and medication to relieve the congestion in his lungs. Put your best nurse onto thirty-minute observations, will you? What's his temperature now?'

'Forty-one degrees,' Maria said, wincing. 'Shall we do sponge baths to bring it down?'

'Yes, please…and we'll give him paracetamol. That should lower it a bit.'

Quickly, Anna prepared the site on Leroy's arm and put in the IV line, carefully checking the fluids she was administering before going on to deal with his oxygen supply.

After a few minutes more, she stepped back and pulled in a deep breath. For the moment she had done all that she could for the boy, but she stroked his head once more and murmured gently to him before she left, 'Try to get some rest, Leroy. The nurse will stay close by, so that you can let her know if you need anything. I'll come and see you in a while.'

Bea came to stand by his bed, and said, 'Bless you, Leroy, my baby. Your mama's going to stay with you as well. I won't be far away from you while you're in here.'

Anna moved quietly away from the bedside, and Carlos went with her.

'You did just fine,' he said approvingly. 'I knew you would.'

Now that the initial spurt of activity was over, Anna was surprised at the way she had been able to push her fears and anxieties to one side. When she had been with the boy, it seemed as though all her professional training had come to the fore, enabling her to deal with the situation.

Now, though, she was beginning to feel shaky all

over again. 'All we can do now is wait,' she said unhappily. 'I wish that this wretched disease could be eradicated once and for all.'

'They're working on a vaccine,' Carlos murmured. 'It should be ready for general use soon. Anyway, there's one consolation…if he comes through this all right, he should have immunity to it for life.'

'Let's hope so.' She gave him a tremulous smile. 'Thanks for staying with me. You made me feel a lot more confident than I might have done otherwise.'

'Any time.' He gave her a quick hug. 'You only have to ask, and I'll be there whenever you need me.'

She absorbed that slowly as they walked back to the office. If only he meant that in all its senses. Somehow she was coming to realise that she would dearly like to have him around as part of her life, come rain, come shine, but that was the last thing on his mind, wasn't it? Had he already pledged himself to Francesca?

She said thoughtfully, 'What did bring you here today? I didn't think to ask you earlier.'

'I thought you might want to hear the news about Joseph. He's improved a lot just these last few days. His chest infection's cleared up, for one thing. I wondered if you would like to go and see him later today.'

'Could I? Oh, yes, that would be wonderful…except that…' She frowned. 'What am I going to do about Leroy?' She was torn both ways.

'It could be days yet before there's any real change. Besides, I can give Maria my phone number, and she'll let us know as soon as anything happens.' His glance flicked over her. 'You won't be able to do any more by staying here, and you'll only make yourself more upset.'

She sighed heavily. 'I suppose that's true enough.' She nodded. 'All right, then. I'd love to go with you.'

'Good. We'll call in at the market on the way and pick up something to cheer him up.'

They set off as soon as Anna's shift finished. Still uneasy about leaving Leroy behind, Anna stared out of the car window and watched the scenery go by without seeing any of it.

Carlos must have sensed her distraction, because he said quietly, 'You're still thinking about him, aren't you? That's the problem with working in a general hospital. You come across difficult situations almost every day of your working life. Have you ever thought of going in for something other than this?'

She was startled enough to come out of her reverie and stare at him. 'And do what?'

He shrugged lightly. 'There must be other work that would give equal satisfaction but without taking such a toll. Have you thought about going in for preventative medicine...working in children's health clinics, maybe?'

'As part of a general practice, you mean?'

'Something like that.'

She shook her head. 'I'm used to hospital work, to dealing with patients who are ill. I think perhaps I need to make more of a difference, to feel that I'm doing something positive to turn the tables.'

He sent her a thoughtful glance. 'You could always come and work at the clinic. You might not find it quite so traumatic. The outcomes are usually better there for patients, partly because we mostly see them before the illness has reached a difficult stage or because they're there to convalesce.'

'Do you need someone at the clinic?'

'I need someone who specialises in paediatrics.'

She was quiet for a moment, then said honestly, 'I'm not sure that I could work in a place where people have to pay for treatment. I've always thought it was wrong that people who are ill shouldn't be able to get the care they need without having to use up their savings or scrimp and scrape to get the best care available.'

He looked at her thoughtfully. 'Some people can afford it,' he murmured. 'They don't want to wait for the health services to work through their waiting lists, especially when it comes to cardiac surgery. It's their choice to jump the queue. They can afford to come to the Caribbean, and then they want to convalesce in beautiful, restful surroundings.'

He smiled at her. 'If you had to choose between staying in an austere ward, where the norm was a quick turnover in patients and harassed nurses and doctors with too little time to deal with you or spending time in a peaceful, luxurious environment, which would you choose?'

She made a wry face. 'I think that's my point. I shouldn't have to choose. If I was ill, I would like to be able to expect the best treatment available without having to pay for it.'

'But that's a dream world, not reality. Health services are overstretched.'

'Maybe.'

They had reached their destination by this time, and Anna could see the village ahead of them, with its neat, colour-washed houses, nestling on the terraced hill slopes.

Carlos parked the car in a dusty lay-by and they set out to explore the various stalls of merchandise that had been set up along the side of the main road.

There was an abundance of bananas, pineapples and guavas, as well as all kinds of fresh vegetables, and at intervals along the way there were kiosks selling hot food, which were attracting quite a crowd.

Anna bought a bag of spiced cakes and a toy boat which she thought Joseph might like to sail in the wash-basin in his room, and Carlos found a carved wooden monkey that climbed a ladder and flipped over when you squeezed the bottom rung.

'He'll love it,' she said with a smile, then asked more seriously, 'When do you think he'll be ready to go home?'

'A couple of weeks, perhaps. I'd like to see him put on a bit more weight first, and I'll be happier when his blood pressure's settled down. He's doing well, though.'

Joseph looked very different from the weak little boy she had seen just a few weeks ago. He gave her a cheeky grin when she walked into his room at the clinic, and went to fetch his action figure.

'Look, Anna. He doesn't have his bandage on any more.'

'Well, that's good news,' she said, giving him a hug. 'And aren't you looking better?'

He nodded gleefully. 'My head doesn't hurt any more now, and I haven't had a nosebleed for ages.'

They were both symptoms that would have been caused by the high blood pressure he had experienced throughout the course of his illness. It was a good sign if he wasn't getting them now.

'Mr Barrantes says if I keep getting stronger, I might be able to go home in a couple of weeks.'

'That's wonderful. That's something to look forward to, isn't it?'

'I'm very pleased with the way you're doing, Joseph,' Carlos put in quietly.

Joseph's smile grew even wider.

They stayed with him for about half an hour, but by then it was clear that he was becoming tired so they left him alone with his parents, who were going to supervise his bedtime. His mother was reading aloud to him as they waved goodbye.

It was getting late when they arrived back at Carlos's house, and Martha had left supper for them in the kitchen before she'd gone off to her own home.

They helped themselves to rice and chicken with freshly sliced red and yellow peppers, and home-made bread spread with golden butter. Afterwards, they sipped coffee and relaxed properly for the first time that day.

'Why don't you go out onto the balcony for a while?' Carlos murmured when they had finished. 'I'll clear this lot away.'

She did as he suggested, going to stand by the parapet and breathe in the warm night air, watching the moon rise in the darkening sky. It was a beautiful night, and the stars were out in full, glittering brightly as though all were well in the world. She sighed softly.

'Are you still worrying about Leroy?' Carlos asked, coming to stand beside her.

'I can't help it,' she muttered huskily, looking out over the harbour, where the lights of the waterfront properties were strung out like a golden necklace. 'I used to see him every day at the apartment, and he would tell me silly jokes and make me laugh, and bring me pictures that he had drawn. I just couldn't bear it if he doesn't pull through.'

He reached for her and turned her around to face him. 'We're doing everything we can. There's nothing more anyone can do.'

'I know that,' she whispered. 'I know you think I shouldn't get involved, but I can't help it.' It wasn't just Leroy that was on her mind. There was Daniel, too, and Sarah back home in England, waiting for better news.

He put his arms around her and drew her close, kissing her lightly on her forehead. 'We all feel like that at times. Sometimes we care so much that it hurts.'

Anna looked at him uncertainly, trying to contain her distress. 'You feel it, too?' But of course he did. He was just better at keeping his feelings hidden than she was.

'You know I do. I wouldn't be human if I didn't feel wrecked if I lose a patient. It happens…you do everything you possibly can, and more, and still sometimes it happens. The key is to keep hope inside you, to feel positive about what you're doing and do your best to transfer that intensity of feeling to your patient.'

'I'll try,' she said in a low voice, and his arms tightened around her.

'I'm here for you,' he said thickly. 'Remember that.' He drew her head down on to his chest, and ruffled her hair lightly, soothing her with slow, gentle movements of his hand across her back.

Carlos's gentleness was her undoing. She loved the feel of him, the warmth, the understanding that flowed from him and smoothed over her senses like honey.

She lifted her head and gazed up at him, and there was a moment of stillness, of some unspoken message winging between them, and somehow their lips met and clung, and the world started spinning on its axis. The kiss went on for a long time, endlessly sweet, filling every part of her with trembling need.

Her hands trailed restlessly over his chest, her fingertips registering the warmth of his skin through his shirt and the heavy thud of his heartbeat.

'Anna, *querida*,' he said raggedly, reluctantly dragging his lips from hers, 'I want to hold you and kiss you, and take away all the pain and heartache, so that you know nothing but me, nothing but what is here and now.'

His lips tracked across her mouth, her cheek, and left a searing trail of fire wherever they touched her sensitive flesh. She moaned softly, wanting him, needing to feel his hands on her, stroking, soothing, making her think of nothing but him.

'I need to touch you,' he muttered huskily. 'You're

so beautiful, so desirable.' His hands were coaxing now, shaping every curve of her body, lingering with exquisite delicacy on the soft swell of her breast, sliding down to stray beneath the thin top she wore. She felt the heat of his long fingers on her bare skin and the sensual glide of his hands as he found her breasts again and traced each burgeoning nub with such tenderness that her head began to swim and she ached for more.

'Let me see you,' he muttered thickly, pushing at the thin material of her top. 'I want to see you, to taste you.'

There was a buzzing in her ears, a ringing sensation as though the blood had rushed to her head and was making her dizzy. She heard his shuddering groan as his head bent lower and his mouth tenderly claimed the taut peak of her breast.

Her breath caught as sensation raced through her entire body and melted her limbs, and then, incredibly, with a muttered curse he was moving away from her, leaving her alone once more, bewildered. Her body was stunned by the shock of rejection, her head was still ringing with the incessant sound of the blood soaring through her veins.

Except that the sound was real. The ringing wasn't just in her head, it was coming from here on the balcony. As she gazed around in bemused dismay, she realised that it was the phone that was making such an unwelcome intrusion.

'*Dios.*' Carlos sucked in air through his teeth. 'I wish I could simply ignore it.'

'You can't,' she said unevenly. 'It might be a patient…it might be news about Leroy.'

Stricken with dismay, she watched him stride over to the table and pick up the phone. His voice was calm and steady as he spoke into the receiver.

Anna looked around, feeling the night air lightly touch her bare skin. Slowly, she started to come to her senses and began to straighten her clothes with fingers that trembled.

She didn't hear much of Carlos's conversation, but when he'd finished the call he said quietly, 'Saskia has gone into labour. The obstetrician wants to do a Caesarean, and she's giving them trouble. I shall have to go and talk to her.'

'Oh, I see… Yes…yes, of course you must.' Anna pulled in a deep breath. 'Is the maternity unit far away?'

He shook his head. 'A couple of miles, that's all. I'll go now.' His eyes were dark and unreadable as he looked at her. 'I don't know how long I'll be. Don't wait up.'

He left within minutes and Anna didn't know whether she ought to be glad or sorry that she had been saved from herself. Would she have regretted what might have happened between them if he'd stayed?

CHAPTER NINE

BY MORNING, Anna had decided that it was probably just as well that they had been interrupted the previous night. It would have been too humiliating if things had gone too far, and then later Carlos had told her it had all been a bad mistake.

After all, he had meant to comfort her, that had been how it had started, and no one could have known that things would get out of hand so quickly.

'*Buenos dias*, Anna.' He came down for breakfast and leaned against the fridge in a lazily masculine way that made her senses leap and immediately turned all her good intentions to ashes. He was wearing dark trousers and a crisp blue shirt that rested flatly against his rib cage and drew her gaze to the tight line of his abdomen.

He had a perfectly muscled body. Just seeing him standing there made her feel hot all over, and hastily she looked away and tried to get her thoughts back together again.

'Good morning.' She returned the greeting and hoped he hadn't noticed the tremor in her voice. 'How is Saskia? I didn't hear you come in last night, or I would have asked you then.'

'I crept in, so as not to wake you,' he murmured. 'She's had a little girl. Both of them are doing well.'

'Oh, I'm glad,' Anna smiled, relieved. 'What happened?'

'It was much as we had expected. The baby still hadn't turned when she went into labour, and was lying in an oblique position. It would have been nigh on impossible to deliver it safely without risking a haemorrhage and putting Saskia's safety on the line as well as that of the baby.'

He winced. 'I did my best to try to persuade her that she ought to do as the doctors were asking and have a Caesarean. I thought I was beginning to make some headway, and then her husband turned up and added his arguments to mine. His flight had come in on time and he had a mad dash to the hospital, but it was a relief all round to see him walk through the door. He managed to talk some sense into her.'

'Why was she so set against the idea of a Caesarean?'

'Some crazy notion that she wouldn't be able to have any more children because of the operation. I don't know how many she's planning, but obviously two aren't going to be enough for her.'

'Even so, to be so adamant when everyone was advising her to go ahead seems odd.'

'That's true, but I don't think she realised that she was putting the baby at risk. We had to explain to her that the baby was tiring and there would be problems if she didn't let them get on with it. That's when she changed her mind.' He chuckled. 'The operation was so easy and so quick that now, of course, she thinks a Caesarean might be the best possible way to have a delivery.'

Anna lifted a cynical brow. 'She might not think that when it takes her a month or so to get over it.'

'She's a strong woman. She'll manage just fine. Besides, my parents have gone to stay with her for a while, so that my mother will be able to help her out a lot in the next few weeks.'

'Has Seb seen his baby sister yet?'

'He saw her first thing this morning, apparently. I phoned to see how Saskia and the baby were doing, and she said they were both feeling fine but tired. Seb told her he thought they ought to have provided him with a baby brother instead of a girl.'

Anna laughed. 'That sounds like Seb. Still, I expect he'll get to like being the man of the house.'

'More than likely.'

Martha came and gave Carlos a nudge. 'Are you going to stay in front of my fridge all morning? I need to get to things, you know.'

'Sorry, Martha.' He moved out of the way, coming to sit opposite Anna at the table. 'Is there any coffee left? I could do with a wake up brew this morning.'

'Plenty. It's freshly made.'

He didn't look as though he needed it. He looked as alert and vital as ever, as though he had just come out of the shower and was invigorated. His hair was still damp and faintly spiky, giving him a sexy, dangerously male appeal.

Just then Anna's phone rang, and she picked it up and heard Sarah's voice.

'Sarah…it's good to hear from you. Are you OK?'

'I'm fine, Anna. I just wanted to let you know that

I'm coming over to see you in a day or so. I'm not sure of my flight details yet.'

'Are you? That's wonderful. I thought you might at some point, but I wasn't expecting it to be quite so soon. I thought you were still having to go to the hospital for check-ups?'

'I am, but this is more important. I can't go on feeling helpless like this any longer. I wondered if you could find me somewhere to stay? Anywhere will do, as long as it's fairly close to Nick's place.'

'I can do that, of course, but how's your leg? Are you up to travelling yet?'

'It's as good as it needs to be. I just have to get over there and see Daniel. I can't bear being stuck here, not able to talk to him or give him a cuddle. I'm missing him so much.'

'I'll find you somewhere, Sarah,' Anna promised. 'I'll let you know the details when you get here.'

'Thanks.'

Sarah cut the call a few minutes later, and Anna started to mull over possibilities in her mind.

'That was your sister?' Carlos asked. 'Is she coming over here?'

She nodded. 'I'm not sure she's up to the journey yet, but she's made up her mind anyway. I'll have to search for somewhere for her to stay. My apartment's still not fixed up, so I might go down to the tourist agency and see what's available.'

'There's no need for you to go to so much trouble. She can stay here.'

Anna looked at him in surprise. 'Are you sure about that?'

'I'm very sure. I'd like to make your sister feel welcome here. There's plenty of room, so she ought to be comfortable enough.'

Anna felt a surge of relief come over her. Even so, she said warily, 'I don't know how long she's planning on staying. You've already done more than we could expect by having me here.'

Amusement flickered in his golden eyes. 'You mean two of you are going to be double trouble? I think I can take the risk.'

'It's just that she's desperate to see Daniel.'

'That's understandable. She must be missing him.'

'She is. She's desperate to have him back with her.' She frowned, and added with a grimace, 'I don't think I could bear it if something like that happened to me. I don't know how she copes. Sarah's brought up Daniel for three years, from when he was a baby, and for a good deal of that time she did it on her own because Nick was away, building up his hotel business in various parts of the world. Now he expects to simply step in and take his son from her.'

It was a heartbreaking situation to be caught up in, and she didn't see how either parent could emerge from it unscathed.

Still toying with the problem, she got to her feet and started to clear away the dishes, until Martha batted her away. 'You go and get yourself off to work, girl. I can clear away the breakfast things.'

Anna retreated to the living room and collected her bag.

Carlos followed, his searching glance travelling over her preoccupied features. 'Have you ever

thought about having children of your own? You
work with them every day, so you must care about
them a lot, and yet you've never spoken about there
being any man in your life in the past. Do think about
being married at some point, with a family of your
own?'

'I've thought about it,' she admitted. 'I don't know
if I'm ready for all that, though. I've watched my
sister's marriage fall apart, and I don't know if I'm
strong enough to go through something like that.
Being emotionally involved with someone leaves you
terribly vulnerable, doesn't it?'

His eyes darkened. 'That's very true.'

He said it in a sober, heartfelt manner, and she
asked quietly, 'Is that how you felt with Fran?'

'I'm not sure how I felt. But I suppose it's never
easy to break up with someone you've been deeply
involved with, is it?'

'Are you glad that she's back?'

'Oh, yes. She was troubled, and she went through
a difficult time, but now she's here where she belongs
and back on course again, and I can give her all the
help and support she needs.'

Where did that leave her? He was being open and
honest with her, and she ought to be thankful for that,
but it left her in a quandary. She was beginning to
realise that her feelings for Carlos went deeper than
she could ever have imagined. No one else could ever
make her feel the way he did, she was sure of it, and
yet there was no future for her with him, was there?
There couldn't be, while he was obviously still seeing

another woman. She would only ever be second best, wouldn't she?

'What do you think Sarah will do about Daniel?' he asked, and she blinked and had to drag her attention back to what he was saying. 'Will she apply to the courts for custody?'

'Probably, if she doesn't make any headway with Nick. I think she would be happier if it didn't come to that, though.'

Carlos nodded. 'She's right. It would be far better if they could settle this between themselves.' He glanced at his watch. 'It's getting late,' he murmured. 'We had better leave for work.'

'Are you at the hospital with me this morning?'

'Yes. I've a ward round to do, and I need to check my operating schedule. I have to fit in an extra surgical procedure next week, and I want to make sure that my timetable is running smoothly.'

'Is it something that has cropped up out of the blue?'

He shook his head. 'No. I'm operating on Fran's little boy.'

She was stunned by what he had told her. She said huskily, 'Fran's child?'

'Ben, yes. He was born with a heart defect. The ductus arteriosus failed to close at birth. He was born prematurely, and his doctor treated him initially with indomethacin, which sometimes helps to close the duct, but it wasn't successful in this case.'

Anna was shocked. 'She must have been desperate to get the right treatment for him. Any mother would be.'

He nodded. 'I said from the first that I would do the operation if she wanted me to. Fran's been through a lot, and when she turned to me for help I wanted to do whatever I could.'

No wonder they were so close to each other. She said unevenly, 'Has he taken a turn for the worse—is that why you're operating now?'

She had come across this type of defect before. The channel between the pulmonary artery and the aorta, two of the large vessels which emerge from the heart, normally closed at birth and allowed blood to be pumped around the body. If the channel didn't close properly, some blood would be directed to the lungs, making the heart work harder to pump sufficient blood to the rest of the body.

'No. He's been ill on and off for the last year with chest infections and there hasn't been a good time to do the operation. We think he's ready now, though, so we're setting it up for next week. If we leave it any longer, we run the risk of him becoming more debilitated than he is already.'

'Is he being admitted to our hospital?'

'No. I'll do the surgery at the clinic. Fran thinks he'll be happier there. She's been bringing him over for visits for the last few weeks to get him used to the place.'

'He isn't very old, is he? It's a lot for any young child to go through.'

'He's two and a half. It's best that he has the surgery now, or his development will be stunted and he runs a high risk of heart failure. Already he's thinner and shorter than he ought to be and he gets short of breath easily, but if the operation's successful, he should start to thrive.'

Anna swallowed hard. 'You're very fond of him, aren't you? I saw the way you were with him that day at the barbecue, and it was fairly obvious then that you think the world of him.'

'I do. After all, he's Fran's child, and he could have been my own, if circumstances had been different. As with Sebastian, I've had a lot of involvement in his upbringing.'

His own child. Anna paled at the thought. Just how deeply did he still care for Fran if he was thinking along those lines?

Even so, she felt a peculiar surge of pity for the woman who had such a sick child. 'It must have been difficult for her,' she said huskily, 'bringing up a child with problems like that, especially if she has had to do it all on her own. The father isn't around, is he? What happened?'

Carlos's eyes darkened, became unreadable. 'Out of the blue, she met someone and fell head over heels in love with him. She knew her family wouldn't approve. He was from the wrong side of the tracks, so to speak, so she went away with him. She hadn't intended to get pregnant, but she was troubled, a little wild, back then, and she made a mistake.'

Anna could only guess how hurt Carlos would have been when all this had happened. She asked huskily, 'Where is the father now?'

'He died in a car accident. He was coming back from a party, late one night, and took a bend too fast. He'd been drinking.'

'I'm sorry.' She moistened her lips with the tip of her tongue. 'That must have been awful for her.'

'It was at the time.' He frowned. 'She tried to go on alone, to make the best of things, but it was hard. Eventually, she came to realise that her family didn't blame her for what she had done, and she came home. She needed their help to look after the child. He was never strong, and she was desperate for their support.'

'And she turned to you. That could have been more of a problem for her…if you had been hurt by what she had done.'

'I've known Fran since she was a child. How could I stop caring about her and wanting to help her just because she had made a mistake?'

Anna felt as though all the breath was seeping out of her. Carlos must love her very much.

That was why he had been seeing so much of Fran lately, staying with her into the early hours of the morning. It wasn't just her son he cared about, it was her, too.

But maybe Fran was still thinking about Ben's father?

That would explain why Carlos had turned to Anna for a few brief moments, wouldn't it? Deep down he still hankered after his first love, but he had to wait for her to get over the other man who still had a place in her heart.

Anna felt ill, thinking about it. She said quietly, 'It must be difficult for you, doing the surgery on a child you know and love.'

'More than you could imagine,' he said tautly.

He moved to the door, ready to set off for work.

They drove separately to the hospital, where he left her to start on her own daily routine while he went off to deal with his own patients.

Anna made a conscious effort to push her troubled thoughts to the back of her mind and went straight to the room where Leroy was being nursed.

'Has there been any change?' she asked Maria.

'Not yet. He's still very ill. His temperature's still too high, and there's been no sign of any real improvement.'

It wasn't the news she wanted to hear. She sat with Bea for a while, trying to offer what encouragement she could, but they both knew they were involved in a waiting game. The boy's recovery would depend very much on how his body responded to the supportive care he was being given. If he couldn't cope and he went into shock, the outcome could be something neither of them wanted to contemplate.

'Keep fighting, Leroy,' Anna whispered, standing by his bed and watching the perspiration filming his brow. He wasn't aware of her being there, and she wondered if her words had reached him at whatever level of consciousness he had fallen to.

He had to get well. She wasn't going to let him die. She checked the volume of fluids they were administering, and took careful note of the urinary output. 'That all looks OK,' she said quietly to Maria. 'Let's make the sponge baths more frequent and see if we can get his temperature down that way.'

At least the two young girls who were being treated for ciguatera poisoning were looking healthier. The diarrhoea was under control now in both children, and the vomiting had stopped.

'I'm pleased with the way they're coming along,' she told the anxious parents. 'If they keep this up, we might be looking at letting them go home in a day or so. We just need to make sure that their temperatures stabilise over a twenty-four-hour period.'

It was a long day. The end of Anna's shift came at last, and she started the drive home, feeling wearier than she had for some time. It was probably her wretched emotions that were to blame for that, rather than any lack of sleep.

With Leroy still making no visible progress, and Carlos wrapped up in his feelings for someone else, she felt like burying her head in her pillow and drowning in self-pity.

She wouldn't do that, though. She was made of stronger stuff, wasn't she? And Sarah was on her way over here and she needed to put on a positive front for her. Sarah had enough problems of her own, without having to listen to Anna's woes.

Anna met her at the airport the following day. She put her arms around her and held her tight, and told her, 'I'm glad you're here. I missed you.'

She scanned Sarah's slim figure. Her sister looked thinner than she remembered. The leg was still in plaster, but at least it was a smaller, more manageable cast.

'Look at you,' she murmured softly. 'You must be tired out after all that travelling. Let's get you back to the house.'

Carlos met them at the door. '*Cómo estas*, Sarah?'

he asked, looking her over and coming forward to give her a helping hand into the living room. 'This leg is taking a long while to heal, isn't it?'

'I'm fine, thanks,' Sarah told him with a smile. 'Yes, I suppose it is taking a while to mend, but that was probably on the cards from the beginning. It was broken in three places.'

'Three places?'

She pulled a face. 'I was knocked down by a car, and I fell awkwardly, which added to the problems, but at least I'm starting to make some progress now. This smaller cast is a relief anyway. It's lighter, for one thing.'

He frowned. 'But it must have been a struggle for you, coming all this way with your leg still not properly healed. How have you managed?'

'I managed well enough. I took taxis mostly to get around, and people have been very kind. Anyway, I'd have coped whatever problems there were. I've waited long enough to get here, and I wasn't going to wait any longer.' Her blue eyes were clear and determined, and anyone could see that she wasn't going to be stopped now. 'Thank you very much for letting me stay here. It's really good of you.'

'*De nada.*' He returned the smile. 'You're welcome. I know how much your problem has been weighing on Anna's mind, and this way I can at least do something to help matters. Feel free to use my house as yours for as long as you're here in the Caribbean. If you want to bring your son here, that's all right by me.'

All at once, Sarah's eyes looked misty, and Anna

guessed she was feeling overwhelmed. 'You're being very kind to me.' Her voice broke. 'I don't know what to say.'

'Then don't say anything. Go and rest your leg and talk to Anna. I shall be out for the rest of the afternoon. I have to go to the clinic and check up on my patients, so you'll have the place more or less to yourselves. I'm sure Anna and Martha will be only too glad to look after you.'

He went out a few minutes later, and left them alone in the house. Anna did what she could to make Sarah feel at home, but after a while she sensed that there was only one thing she could really do to help. She left Sarah alone with the phone so that she could call Nick in private.

At the hospital a few days later, Carlos asked, 'How are things going with Sarah and her son? Has she made any headway?'

Anna shook her head. 'None so far. Nick isn't letting her near him. He hasn't even let her talk to him on the phone.' She grimaced. 'The way he's going, he's not leaving her much alternative but to go ahead and pursue things through the courts, is he? I suppose he's not too bothered about that either. Presumably he thinks that because he has money, he'll win hands down.'

'Possibly,' Carlos murmured, 'though it isn't necessarily the case that he would win. After all, if they divorce, he'll have to make her a fair settlement, and the courts may decide that she has the greater claim.'

She looked at him quizzically. 'I thought you were

on Nick's side in this. Does this mean you're changing your mind about who should have custody?'

'Not at all. I've said all along that there are no rights or wrongs about this, just heartache if they don't get it sorted out.'

Anna sighed. 'Nick's been letting me visit Daniel recently, but now I feel as though I can't go and see him. It wouldn't be fair on Sarah. This whole thing's a terrible mess.'

'You shouldn't be taking any of this on yourself,' he said with a frown. 'You have enough to deal with at work.' He gave her a searching glance. 'Is there any news on Leroy?'

'Nothing,' she said in a small voice. 'We just keep on waiting and hoping.' She pulled in a deep breath. 'This is the danger time, when shock could develop, so I've asked Maria to increase the observations and let me know as soon as there's any change.'

He nodded. 'A decreasing platelet count and a rising haematocrit would indicate an increased possibility of impending shock. Let's hope it doesn't come to that.'

He scanned her face briefly. 'If you feel up to it, Joseph was asking if you would be coming to see him before he goes home. I said I would ask you. I'm thinking of releasing him in a couple of days.'

'I'll come over tomorrow, after work, if that's all right.'

He nodded. 'That should be fine. I'll tell him that you'll try to make it, barring emergencies.'

'When will you be operating on Ben?'

'Later today. I'll be at the clinic for some time

because I want to keep a careful eye on him for a while afterwards.'

She could understand that. She watched him walk away, and knew that if Ben had been her child there would have been no one she would have trusted more to see him through this.

'He's looking as though he has plenty on his mind,' Tom said, catching up with her as she went to chase up the results of some blood tests.

'He's going over to the clinic to operate on Francesca's little boy,' Anna told him. 'I think he cares an awful lot about what happens to him.'

'It won't be the first child he's taken a special interest in. There have been quite a number over the short time I've known him. I don't think he can help himself, especially if the parents are in a desperate situation. He often operates free of charge, you know, and arranges to have all their after-care done for nothing at all if it means the child can have a new lease of life.'

'Does he?' Anna was stunned. 'I didn't know that. He didn't give as much as a hint.'

'He wouldn't. It's not something he talks about. It's not his way. I only found out because some of the patients told me. He's a very private man when it comes down to it, and I don't suppose any of us really knows him all that well.'

She was quiet for a moment, taking it all in. And to think Carlos had actually told her that she was too involved with her patients to make a good doctor…when all the time he was every bit as sensitive as she was. Just thinking about it brought a lump to her throat.

Tom was watching her, a faint frown tugging at his brow, and she braced herself and asked him carefully, 'How are you getting on with your studying? Are you taking the exams soon?'

He made a face. 'Next week. I think I'm not doing too badly. I'll be glad when it's all over, though, and life can get back to normal.'

Anna gave a shaky laugh. 'Don't we all think that?' She didn't think her life would ever get back to normal now that she had come to know Carlos. He filled her thoughts every waking moment, and even her dreams, too.

Carlos didn't come home that night, and she guessed he had stayed over at the clinic. Had things not gone as he had planned? Anna fretted a little, wanting to know, wanting to be there with him, but she couldn't do that, could she? She was an outsider in that trio, and she would simply be in the way.

All the same, she had said that she would go and see Joseph, and she meant to keep her word. She made quick preparations the next evening after work, worrying a little about whether Sarah was going to be all right while she was away.

'I'll be fine,' Sarah told her. 'I'll watch a video, or perhaps I'll read a book.' Anything to take her mind off her fruitless attempts to see her son, Anna guessed, and she could have wept for her.

Just as she was about to leave the house, though, there was a knock at the door, and when she went to open it, her mouth dropped open in astonishment. Nick stood there with Daniel at his side.

'I came to see Sarah,' he said, and Anna stood back, wide eyed, and let him in. She gave Daniel a hug.

'Your mummy is going to be so happy to see you,' she told him. 'She's in the living room over there. She's been waiting for such a long time to give you a cuddle.'

'Over there?' Daniel echoed, then with a whoop of glee he ran off towards the double doors and disappeared into the room.

Nick and Anna exchanged glances. 'Have you had a change of heart?' she asked.

He gave an awkward shrug. 'I suppose, in the end, I had no choice but to come,' he said. 'Daniel has been asking for her. I ran out of things to tell him.'

Anna put her arms around him and squeezed him tightly, a blur of tears masking her eyes. 'You did the right thing,' she muttered huskily. 'I'm really glad you came.'

He looked uncomfortable at being hugged, and at first he was stiff in her embrace. After a moment, though, he relaxed and said with a wry face, 'I expect we'll sort something out. You and your sister are two of a kind. You don't give up easily, do you?'

'Not easily, no,' she murmured.

'Carlos told me that neither of you would let it go. He told me I was a fool to try to keep Daniel from his mother.'

'He said that?' Anna looked at him, surprised, and stepped back a fraction.

'More than that, in fact,' Nick said, looking chastened. 'Most of it not repeatable in present company.' He grimaced. 'I suppose he had a point. I don't want this dragged through the courts when maybe we could come to some kind of agreement.'

'I think you're being very wise,' she murmured unsteadily, still fazed by the knowledge that Carlos had intervened. 'Try to keep calm and talk things through with Sarah. I'm sure that somehow you'll be able to work it out for the best for both of you.'

A muscle flexed in his jaw. 'We have to try.' He gave an almost imperceptible nod in her direction, then straightened his shoulders and started to walk towards the living room.

Anna crossed her fingers that they would manage to keep from arguing for the next hour or so. She wasn't going to be here to act as referee.

Joseph was waiting for her in the patients' day room when she arrived at the clinic a short time later. He was playing a computer game, and when he looked up at her his face was glowing with health.

'Look at you,' she said with a smile. 'There's colour in your cheeks, and I'm certain you've put weight on. You look so much better.'

'I am. I'm going home tomorrow. Mr Barrantes says I'm as fit as a fiddle and he can't think of any reason to keep me here any longer.' He grinned at her. 'That's good news, isn't it?'

'It's brilliant news. The very best.'

'I've made him a card to say thank you for looking after me.' He reached into his dressing-gown pocket and pulled it out. 'Look, here it is. Do you think he'll like it? It's a picture of him, with a big smile on his face, and I'm there in my bed, saying, "I'm better now."'

Anna looked down at the picture, drawn with a seven-year-old's innocent hand, an interpretation of two figures who were clearly colourful and impressive. 'He'll love it,' she told him.

He smiled broadly. 'Good.'

She stayed with him for a while longer, then left when his mother came to fetch him for his bedtime drink.

Joseph's nurse, Freya, met her as she was leaving the room.

'Mr Barrantes said that you might be coming here this evening,' she greeted Anna. 'You've seen Joseph? He's doing very well, isn't he?'

'Very well,' Anna murmured. 'He looked so different from the way he was at the hospital a few weeks ago.'

'Yes, that's true. Mr Barrantes has taken very good care of him. He's a wonderful surgeon, you know. Are you going to have a word with him before you go? He's in the office, I think. Just along the corridor.' She pointed towards a set of fire doors. 'Through there, and it's the second room on the right.'

'If he's not too busy?' She would dearly like to know how Ben's surgery had gone.

She wondered how Francesca would be coping. The child was very young, and any mother would be traumatised by something like this.

The defect was a fairly common one—eight per cent of congenital heart defects involved the duct.

Usually, with the kind of operation Carlos would have performed, there was little risk, but it seemed odd that he hadn't come back to the house last night, and she hadn't seen him at all today.

'He had a hefty operating schedule yesterday and today, and he wanted to stay and check on the post-operative procedures. I think he might be free now, though.'

'The little boy, Ben, who had his operation yesterday afternoon—is he all right?'

'He's in Intensive Care. As far as I know, everything went well. I'm afraid I can't tell you any more...unless you're a relative?'

Anna shook her head. 'No. I'm just a friend of Mr Barrantes, that's all.'

A friend. Was she anything more to him than that? She walked along the corridor and through the fire doors, slowing down when she came to the office. The door was partly open and she would have gone in there, except that she could see that Carlos wasn't alone.

She stood very still, frozen to the spot. Francesca was with him, and they had their arms around each other in an intimate embrace. Carlos was bending his head to hers and all of a sudden Anna couldn't bear to see any more. She didn't want to see him kissing her. It was too much to take in.

Her heart was hammering like a wild thing in her chest and she wanted to run down the corridor and get out of this place as fast as she could. She felt sick, the nausea rising up in her like an unwelcome tide.

What had she expected? That Carlos would simply forget his former love and turn to her?

That was just a dream, a figment of her imagination, conjured up in a moment of moonlight madness. He had always loved Francesca, he had made no secret of it.

Now that her son was ill he was there for her, ready to take care of him, and to support her. They were probably closer to each other now than they had ever been.

Anna turned silently away and stumbled back the way she had come. She had to get out of this place quickly, before she broke down completely and humiliated herself.

CHAPTER TEN

'How is Leroy this morning?' Anna asked Maria. She looked at the boy, still lying in bed in a debilitated condition, and guessed the answer before Maria spoke.

'There's been very little change, except that his breathing seems a fraction easier with the medication to relieve the congestion on his lungs.'

'That's something, at least.' Anna frowned. 'You're doing a great job. Keep up the sponge baths and keep an eye on his skin condition. We don't want him suffering from bedsores as well as everything else.'

She finished off her ward rounds and with lunchtime looming she thought about going to find a coffee in the cafeteria, more for the chance to retreat from the world for a while than for any thought of food. She needed time to think, to get over what she had seen last night.

Carlos had left the house early that morning, before she had come down for breakfast, and Sarah had been full of her evening with Daniel. It was good to see her sister looking so animated and happy. It helped to numb some of her own pain.

One of the nurses from Casualty came to find her just as she was heading for the lift.

'We've a young girl who's just been brought in,

showing signs of shock after a jellyfish sting. Would you come and have a look at her?'

'Yes, I'll do that.' Anna mentally said goodbye to a few moments of peace and followed the nurse to the examination cubicle. Jellyfish stings could be nasty. Some jellyfish were really large and dangerous, and could bring about very unpleasant reactions.

Her patient, a young girl of around eleven, had been vomiting, and now she had collapsed back onto the bed, sweating and obviously in a good deal of pain.

'Hello, Caitlin,' Anna greeted her. 'I'm Dr Somerville. Would you like to tell me what happened?'

'I went for a swim at the beach,' Caitlin answered jerkily. 'Then, when I was coming back to the shore, I stood up and I must have trodden on something.' She paused to pull in a shaky breath. 'Will you get it out for me? Please, get it out…it really hurts.'

'Of course. I'll just have a look at your foot, and then we'll see what we can do to make you feel more comfortable. It's your right foot, is that the one?'

'Yes.'

The sole of the foot was badly swollen and inflamed, and the tentacles of the jellyfish were still in place. Looking at them, Anna could see that they were from a particularly vicious type of creature.

'Better not touch them with our bare hands,' she muttered to the nurse who hovered nearby. 'The stinging capsules discharge their venom when they're touched, and we don't want to risk any more damage. We'll inactivate them first, and then try to remove them. We'll need a half-and-half solution of baking soda and water.'

The nurse went off to get the solution, and Anna told her patient, 'It looks as though you've been attacked by a sea nettle jellyfish, Caitlin. We're going to put your foot into a solution that should stop the stingers from doing any more damage, and then we'll be able to remove the tentacles.'

'Just make it quick,' Caitlin said through her teeth.

'I'll give you something for the pain,' Anna murmured, and dealt with that while she was waiting for the nurse to come back. She used an analgesic, and also gave the girl an antivenom medication.

As soon as the nurse arrived with the solution, Anna helped the girl to put her foot into the bath and made sure that she kept it there until it had done its job.

Then she carefully set about removing the tentacles one by one with tweezers. When she had finished at last she said, 'There, that's done. You should start to feel better soon, but I think we'll keep you here for an hour or so, Caitlin, just to make sure that everything's settled down.'

Turning to the nurse, she drew her to one side and added quietly, 'I think she'll probably be all right now, but we need to put her on the side ward and watch for any signs of worsening shock. Look out for any breathing difficulties, convulsions or collapse. The parents can stay with her.'

'Will do.'

Anna went off in search of coffee.

The cafeteria was emptying now, as the lunch hour

faded. Helping herself to a cappuccino, Anna went to find a table by the window where she could be quiet and solitary.

Her peace was short-lived.

'Anna…I wondered if I would find you here. I've been looking for you.'

She looked up to see Carlos standing by her table. He put his tray down and slid into the seat opposite her.

'Freya told me that you had been to visit Joseph yesterday. I meant to come and join you, but I was tied up for most of the evening with other things.'

She almost winced. She knew very well what those things were, and she didn't want to dwell on them, even for a minute. She said, 'He was looking well. You must be pleased.'

'I am. It's always good to see patients on the mend.'

'How is little Ben?' she asked in spite of herself. 'Did everything go well with him?'

'It was straightforward enough. Being so young, it always looks worse afterwards than it perhaps is, with tubes and monitoring equipment and so on. He's making a good recovery now, though.'

'I'm glad.' She stirred the coffee, making swirls in the frothy topping. Carlos looked in good form today, and why wouldn't he? Wasn't everything going his way?

'Are you all right?' he asked. 'You look preoccupied. Is anything wrong? Is it Leroy?'

'No, there's been very little change in his condition. I wish there was more I could do for him but, apart from supportive care and keeping alert for any major changes, there's nothing I can do. It's frustrating.' She wasn't going to tell him what else was going on in her mind. It would be too painful and she couldn't bear to see pity in his eyes.

'Sometimes it's as well to do nothing. Let nature do the work.'

'Maybe.' She glanced up at him. 'I didn't know that you were going to talk to Nick. Whatever you said to him seemed to have a profound effect…he came over last night with Daniel, and it looks as though he and Sarah have talked properly for the first time in months. Sarah was really happy this morning.'

'Was she?' He smiled. 'I'm glad about that. It seemed such a terrible situation to have the two of them at loggerheads and the child caught up in the middle of it. Have they come to any agreement?'

'I don't think they've got quite that far just yet. Just an acceptance that they'll both spend some time with Daniel.'

'Do you think she'll eventually go back to England with the child?'

'I expect so. Our family are over there most of the time, and Sarah will probably want to go back to work there at some stage.'

'What about you? What will you do when the work at the hospital comes to an end?'

'I don't know. I haven't made up my mind yet.' She had been putting off making a decision about that. Perhaps in the back of her mind she had been hoping that she might be able to stay, but now she wasn't sure she could do that. How could she live here and work with Carlos, knowing that he was in love with someone else? 'I'll probably go back to England with Sarah, and find myself a job in a hospital close to where she lives.'

She glanced down at her watch. 'I ought to be getting back. I want to check on Leroy.'

'I'll come with you.'

They walked back to the ward together, and went to stand by the boy's bed.

'His breathing was a little easier this morning,' Anna said quietly, 'and some of the swelling has gone down. I don't think his liver is as enlarged as it was. Those are all good signs. I just wish we could be sure that this is a turning point.'

Carlos frowned, looking at the temperature chart. 'Perhaps we can,' he murmured. 'Look, there's been a drop here of one degree.' He looked at her, his eyes creasing in a smile. 'It doesn't sound a lot, but I think we could be making some headway at last.'

She came to look at the chart with him, and he put an arm around her and hugged her close. 'It's a first sign, nothing more, but it's a good sign, Anna.'

She closed her eyes and absorbed the news, conscious of his closeness, of the warmth of his body next to hers, the reassuringly steady thud of his heartbeat.

'We've waited such a long time,' she whispered. 'It has to be the start of something good.'

Carlos's pager sounded just then, and he groaned, checking it. 'I'll have to answer that,' he said quietly. 'I'll come back and see you later on.'

She nodded. 'I'll be here.' Now that she had seen

this first breakthrough, she was going to watch Leroy until there was stronger improvement. She wanted to be here when that happened.

Carlos returned, as he had promised, though it was much later on in the afternoon when he came to find Anna in the patients' lounge. She had stayed on long after her shift should have ended.

'Maria said you were in here,' he murmured.

Bea was restlessly moving about the room, alternately sitting down and getting to her feet, not knowing what to do with herself.

'Go and get yourself something to eat,' Anna said firmly after a while. 'If there's going to be any change in him, he'll need you to be strong and on top of things. You won't be able to help him at all if you're feeling agitated and weak.'

After a few more circuits of the room, Bea gave in. 'I'll be back in ten minutes,' she said. 'You tell him.'

'I'll tell him. Off you go.'

Carlos watched Bea walk away, and came to put an arm around Anna's shoulders. 'Let's go and have a look at him, shall we?'

Leroy was sleeping peacefully when they went into his room and Anna could see the change in him straight away. 'His temperature's dropped again,' she said with a smile. Her gaze meshed with Carlos's. 'He's going to be all right, Carlos. He's going to get well.'

Leroy stirred and mumbled something, and Anna leaned closer, trying to catch what he was saying.

'I can't make it out properly,' she told Carlos, shaking her head, 'but I think he said something about ice cream.'

'Then he's definitely on the mend,' he said with a grin. 'When his appetite's back and his temperature stays down for twenty-four hours without antipyretics, we'll know he's well on his way to full recovery.'

They stayed to tell Bea the good news, and once Leroy had begun to wake up properly and had managed to sit up a little in bed, Maria went off to the hospital kitchen to find a supply of ice cream.

It was about an hour after that when they finally thought about going home.

'I don't think I want to go back yet,' Anna said softly. 'I'm too restless to want to do normal, routine things.'

'Shall we go to the beach?' Carlos murmured. 'We could take a walk along the bay.'

He took her to a nearby cove, where they wandered aimlessly across the smooth sand and listened to the waves lapping on the shore. The sun was setting and casting a golden glow over the palm-fringed beach, and when Anna looked out over the crystal-clear waters of the warm Caribbean Sea, she saw the rays reflected in the shimmering water. Further out, yachts lazed at anchor, their sails wafting lightly in the faint breeze.

'It's so restful here,' she murmured. 'It's beautiful.'

'And yet you're thinking of leaving all this behind you.' He drew her down onto the warm sand, and they sat, side by side, looking out over the blue waters of the peaceful lagoon. 'Can't I persuade you to stay? You're a good doctor, Anna. We need people like you out here. I could find you a place at the clinic if you'd only think about it.'

'I—'

She frowned and started to speak, but he cut in, saying quickly, 'I know you said that you don't like working in a place where people have to pay for treatment, but we can work around that. I'm going to set up a wing especially for free patients, a children's unit, and I need someone to be in overall charge of it. With your paediatric experience, you'd be ideal.' He searched her face for her reaction. 'Will you at least consider it?'

'It sounds perfect,' she said softly, 'but I'm not sure that I could stay here.' It would hurt too much to see Carlos every day and know that he wanted someone else. She wasn't strong enough to cope with that, was she?

'Because of Sarah and Daniel? Would you still feel the same if I found them a place where they could stay? A little house…somewhere for Sarah to call home whenever she's here. She could stay in it permanently, or she could come and go between here and England and it would always be hers.'

Anna's green eyes widened. 'Why would you do something like that?'

'Why not? I can afford it, and it would help to resolve part of her problem. She and Nick would be able to see Daniel whenever they wanted—I could even find her a job if that's what she wants.'

'I meant, why would you want to do this? I know you're generous—Tom told me about the work you do already for people at the clinic for nothing—and I know how much you care for people, but why is it so important to you that Sarah has a home here?'

His gaze was steady. 'I want you to stay here, and I'll do anything I can to persuade you not to leave, and that includes persuading your sister to accept my offer. I want you here with me. Is that too difficult to understand?'

His offer was breathtakingly tempting, but she was totally confused by it. 'There are lots of doctors… paediatricians…who would do just as good a job as me. Any one of them might want to work at the clinic.'

He looked pained. 'Are you turning me down?'

'I'm trying to understand.'

'Why is it so hard for you to accept that I care about you, that I want you to stay here with me? I need you, Anna. I can't begin to think about what life will be like if you leave me.'

He put his arm around her and held her close. 'Don't say no to me, Anna…please, don't do that. Won't you say that at least you'll think about it?'

Anna watched the sun sink lower in the sky, mesmerised by the gentle motion of the palm trees swaying lightly in the warm breeze. None of this was real, was it? He wasn't really saying what she had thought he was saying.

'But you'll have Fran with you—she'll be here for you. She needs you. Why should it matter so much if I go away? You love her, you said you loved her.'

'Yes, it's true, I've always loved Fran. We practically grew up together. But she's not you. It's not the same at all. At first I might have wondered what my true feelings were for Fran, but a long while ago I realised that they were more protective than anything else…brotherly, if you like. She's like a sister to me.'

Anna stared at him, her eyes large with surprise. 'You never once said that she was like a sister to you. You said that you were going to be married.'

'Did I?' Carlos frowned. 'I might have said that we were talking about getting married, or that it was expected that we would marry. That's something else altogether.' He shook his head. 'Believe me, I've never seriously wanted to marry Fran.'

He paused, studying her face. 'Our parents, now, they had other ideas. They're very traditional, and it seemed to them that we would be a good match, that our marriage would bring the two estates together in a partnership that could only be good all round.'

His mouth twisted. 'Unfortunately for them, we had other ideas.'

'Did Francesca feel the same? She never wanted you?'

'Not as a husband, but she couldn't tell her parents that there was no hope. They were making so many plans. They had it all worked out, and even though I told them that I wasn't son-in-law material, they didn't believe it, or they didn't want to believe it. They thought they could persuade us to change our minds. Perhaps to a certain extent we even considered it at one time…a marriage of convenience that would suit everyone. But it wouldn't have been right. We both knew that. Anyway, Fran met someone else, and decided to run away.'

His gaze searched her face, reading the doubt in her eyes. 'Don't you know that it's you I love?'

'But I saw you together,' she said unhappily. 'That evening when I came to the clinic to see Joseph, you were holding her in your arms.' Even now, it hurt her to think about it.

'Why didn't you come and talk to me?' He frowned. 'I would have told you that there was nothing going on between us.'

Anna wasn't convinced. 'It looked to me as though there was.'

'Fran was upset. She'd been to see Ben after the operation, and he had tubes coming out of him and drips in place, and she was afraid that he was very ill, that he might not get better. She was very emotional. Ben's only two years old, and very tiny. He looked helpless and she couldn't cope with that.'

Anna's brow furrowed. 'I suppose I can understand that. I don't think I could cope if it was my child lying there, even though I see sick children all the time. It's bad enough when they're your patients, but if they're your own flesh and blood... Poor Fran. Is she going to be all right? You said Ben was recovering well, didn't you?'

'He'll be fine, and so will Fran. She's stronger now, and she'll get her life back together.' Carlos drew her into his arms. 'It's you I'm concerned about. I want to know that you're going to be here with me. I love you, Anna. I want you to stay with me, live with me, be my wife.'

'You do?'

'More than anything.' He looked at her anxiously,

and said in a roughened voice, 'You do care for me, don't you? You must, or why else would it bother you if I was with Fran?' He gently brushed her cheek with his fingers, and murmured thickly, 'I'll make you happy, Anna. I'll do whatever I can to make sure that you never regret staying here. That's a promise. Just say that you'll stay, and that you'll marry me.'

'But how can I? What will your parents say? After they pinned all their hopes on Francesca, they might not like me at all...'

'They'll love you, just as Saskia loves you. Anyway, it was Fran's parents who were most keen.'

'But we're worlds apart...'

'You *are* my world,' he said huskily. 'Without you I'm nothing, I have nothing—don't you understand that? Say that you'll marry me.'

Anna's mouth curved in a smile. 'I will, I—'

She didn't get to say any more, though, because Carlos kissed her then with a passionate intensity that took her breath away. He eased her down onto the soft, cushioning sand and she cradled his face in her hands, her fingers exploring the craggy contours with love and need.

'I love you,' she whispered, and she felt his shuddery sigh against her breast as he held her tightly as though he would never let her go. He rained kisses over her nose, her cheeks, her throat, then looked down at her with warmth and tenderness in his eyes.

'You and I will have such a good life together,' he murmured against her cheek. 'I'll always love you, Anna...that's my promise.'

As the moon silvered the sky and cast its powerful magic over them, Anna smiled up at him and knew that his promise would last for all time.

Modern Romance™
...seduction and
passion guaranteed

Tender Romance
...love affairs that
last a lifetime

Sensual Romance™
...sassy, sexy and
seductive

Blaze
...sultry days and
steamy nights

Medical Romance™
...medical drama on
the pulse

Historical Romance™
...rich, vivid and
passionate

29 new titles every month.

*With all kinds of Romance for
every kind of mood...*

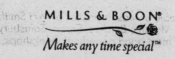

MILLS & BOON®

Makes any time special™

MAT4

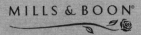

Medical Romance™

GUILTY SECRET by Josie Metcalfe

Part 2 of Denison Memorial Hospital

It started the moment Nick set eyes on Dr Frances Long. More than sexual, it was soul deep. Then Frankie was introduced to the surgery's new GP—her colleague's fiancé, Nick Johnson! Frankie couldn't live with the guilt and neither could Nick. But until they were free to be together, how could anyone live happily ever after?

PARTNERS BY CONTRACT by Kim Lawrence

Dr Phoebe Miller is settling in well to her new practice—until senior partner Dr Connor Carlyle returns from his holiday and sparks begin to fly! Connor was Phoebe's first love, but he'd been bound to another woman. Now Connor is free again he wants to keep Phoebe as his partner in the practice—and in his life!

MORGAN'S SON by Jennifer Taylor

As Morgan stood by her bed with Tomàs in his arms Katrina felt her dream of adopting Tomàs with Morgan, and reviving their marriage after four years, evaporate. Morgan had always opposed adoption and her only hope had been to persuade him gently, slowly. Little chance of that now—unless Tomàs had worked his charms on Morgan too…

On sale 1st February 2002

Treat yourself this Mother's Day to the ultimate indulgence

3 brand new romance novels and a box of chocolates

= only £7.99

Available from 18th January

2 FREE

books and a surprise gift!

We would like to take this opportunity to thank you for reading this Mills & Boon® book by offering you the chance to take TWO more specially selected titles from the Medical Romance™ series absolutely FREE! We're also making this offer to introduce you to the benefits of the Reader Service™—

- ★ FREE home delivery
- ★ FREE gifts and competitions
- ★ FREE monthly Newsletter
- ★ Exclusive Reader Service discount
- ★ Books available before they're in the shops

Accepting these FREE books and gift places you under no obligation to buy, you may cancel at any time, even after receiving your free shipment. Simply complete your details below and return the entire page to the address below. *You don't even need a stamp!*

YES! Please send me 2 free Medical Romance books and a surprise gift. I understand that unless you hear from me, I will receive 4 superb new titles every month for just £2.49 each, postage and packing free. I am under no obligation to purchase any books and may cancel my subscription at any time. The free books and gift will be mine to keep in any case.

M2ZEA

Ms/Mrs/Miss/Mr ....Initials....................................
BLOCK CAPITALS PLEASE

Surname ....

Address ....

....

....Postcode................................

Send this whole page to:
UK: FREEPOST CN81, Croydon, CR9 3WZ
EIRE: PO Box 4546, Kilcock, County Kildare (stamp required)

Offer valid in UK and Eire only and not available to current Reader Service subscribers to this series. We reserve the right to refuse an application and applicants must be aged 18 years or over. Only one application per household. Terms and prices subject to change without notice. Offer expires 30th April 2002. As a result of this application, you may receive offers from other carefully selected companies. If you would prefer not to share in this opportunity please write to The Data Manager at the address above.

Mills & Boon® is a registered trademark owned by Harlequin Mills & Boon Limited.
Medical Romance™ is being used as a trademark.